Falen, Semper Fi

To Kimberly
Best
Jim Mackie

Other novels by James MacKrell

The Bandit Series: Down from the Mountain

James MacKrell
✉ jmackrell@thebanditproject.com

For more information, please visit our website at
www.thebanditproject.com

JMK PRESS

Copyright © 2014 James M. MacKrell, Inc.

ISBN-13:978-1499342383
ISBN-10:1499342381

DEDICATION

It is with great pleasure I dedicate this Bandit Book, "Falen: Semper Fi" to a man without whom these books would have never been written. Since no man is an island, I include his wife Judie Rae Manuel in this dedication because of her tireless effort in providing the right information about this subject matter and the fact through her, Walt added a lot about Ranching and Montana.

I learned to greatly respect this couple for their hard work, their integrity, and their willingness to protect an American Way of Life, called Ranching.

Walt was truly a Montana Cowboy. From his birth in 1946 until his untimely death in 2011, Walt Manuel was a man of the land. This couple's family date back generations in Big Sky country and everything you think about when you envision that sprawling territory is true about the Manuel's.

Both taught me about the wonderful canine breed, the Australian Shepherd. In fact, Falen the daughter of their wonderful sire Warner, and granddaughter of his famous father Bandit, is the star of this book and is at my feet even now as I write. I only hope to portray these dogs and the people who love and depend on them as well as Judie and Walt have with their lives.

Judie is still as vibrant as the first time we spoke. Her heart is a bit heavier as she moves on in life without her beloved Walt.

I hope Walt is proud of our efforts. You are missed by us all.

May you forever rest in peace.

ACKNOWLEDGMENTS

After I finish writing a novel, my favorite task is thanking all of the people who've made the writing process possible. For *"Falen: Semper Fi"* the list is long. As in my dedication I will be forever indebted to Walt and Judie Manuel for their encouragement and willingness to make my dream a reality. *The Bandit Series* came to life because Walt and Judie said yes to my invitation to become technical advisors on my first book, *"Down from the Mountain."*

It was through Judie's enthusiasm for the project that I got to meet Anne Shope and her wonderful family. She and her daughter Stephanie Shope McDaniel spent hours proofing the books and making some excellent suggestions. Anne is a Hall Fame Breeder and a judge of conformation, rally and obedience. Her husband Steve is a judge of Stock and Herding dogs. Both supplied me with Aussie behavioral tendencies and helped me develop the nature of the fictional dogs to the highest standard of the breed.

I would love to list all of the Aussie Breeders who encouraged me and offered valuable suggestions but the list is long! I do want to make special mention of two gals, Teri Carver and Jarilyn Pusz – so many thanks to you both!

My friend Jeanne Joy Hartnagle-Taylor, who is a published author, subject matter expert and stockdog clinician, offered me encouragement and inspiration through my writing process. Her books set the standard for Herding Dog breeds.

The idea for *"Falen, Semper Fi"* came from an article I happened upon when surfing the Internet. *"The Role of Service Dog Training in the Treatment of Combat-related PTSD." (www.Healio.com)* I was introduced to an amazing organization called the Warrior Canine Connection (WCC), a nonprofit based in Brookville, MD that enlists "wounded warriors" with PTSD and Traumatic Brain Injury (TBI) in the training of service dogs for fellow veterans as a therapeutic intervention. Their work is truly inspiring. I encourage you to learn more about them at www.WarriorCanineConnection.org.

One of my own physicians, Dr. Matthew McCauley, introduced me to the Intrepid Fallen Hero's Fund. Another not-for-profit organization that strives to make the healing process of our wounded warriors and their families, easier and more productive. Again, I encourage you to learn more about IFHF by visiting their website: www.FallenHeroesFund.org.

This novel and my other *"Down from the Mountain"* would not have reached the computer without a service I subscribe to called Auto Crit. Any person writing anything at any time should certainly avail themselves of this marvelous web-based tool. You can find them at www.AutoCrit.com

And of course I offer my heartfelt thanks to all of the wonderful people who assisted me in the editorial process. First and foremost, my daughter Catie MacKrell, who wears many hats: graphic designer, publication formatter, and marketing guru. "You da best, Scoot!" And my dear proof reader and maven of English grammar, my wife Cathy Scanlin MacKrell, without whom I couldn't draw a breath. Also those who selflessly spent their time reading and offering suggestions - my sincere thanks! Sue Townsend Smith from Doberstat Dobermans who I depended on for her good wishes as well as keen eye. Ed and Jean Mills who read every page and kept encouraging me throughout. My dear friend and comrade Michael Crew, who labored alongside me through this endeavor – thank you for your patience and friendship.

Lastly, to all of the Dogs in my life. Each has taught me so much about life and love. We share a tiny fragile world and we need to lean on each other as we make our way through it.

Falen, Semper Fi

Falen One

The sun's rays bake the skin on my stomach in such a wonderful way, I think I might lay here on the porch forever. When I get too warm, thankfully, a mountain breeze swirls around the side of the house and makes my hair ruffle and cool's my soul. This summer weather always brings out the best in me, as if there is ever anything wrong with my attitude or manner, but I might be a tad prejudiced. I do love this wonderful place the Spirit of the Day and Night has given me, as I reminisce about past adventures and daydream in this warm, lazy Montana sun.

Let me introduce myself. I'm Falen, daughter of Warner and Jenny, and I'm a full- blooded Australian Shepherd.

In case you've neglected to observe, I'm one of the most gorgeous examples of my breed; everyone, humans and dogs alike, tell me so.

I'm most proud of the fact I that resemble my Mother, Jenny, in size, and coat color.

We're both what is called in Aussie talk, Red Tri's, red with white and copper trim. I want my heart to mirror my brother, Bandit's. His heart is the size of the Big Sky country; full up with promise and strength, welcoming, strong and powerful. I wish I might be as brave and wise as he always seems to be.

Excuse me a minute, something is biting me behind the ear and my back paw is trying to set the record for the number of times it can whip up a fury on the side of my head. There, that's better. Now where was I? Oh yes, I was extolling the many virtues of me being me. I am a proud Australian Shepherd bred in the tradition of herding dogs dating back to the Mountains of Spain, France and Italy. However, I am pure American through and through.

My brother Bandit and I were born under unique circumstances, if you can call being lost in a blizzard and holed up in a small grotto in the side wall of a deep ravine unique. During a blinding snowstorm our Mother got separated from our shepherd, Javier; and when it's time to be born, it's time! It doesn't matter whether we're cozy at home or as it happened, stuck in an icy cavern in the middle of the Absaroka wilderness, we got born. Weeks later, after our mother almost wasted away keeping us secure and fed, a freak weather condition called a Chinook wind rose out of the west. It melted the snow enough for Javier Coronado to be able to search for and rescue his Jenny, and to his surprise a red girl puppy. My brother, Bandit, sleeping and hidden in the back of the gully was overlooked as Javier pulled mother and me out of the hole. Don't worry, life for my brother, although quite a journey had a happy ending. A Wolf called Sheena raised Bandit and brought him

'Down from the Mountain', but that's another incredible story.

Since I've been three winters old I've lived with my wonderful master, Rick Gonzales. I met him at his homecoming party when he returned from a war in Afghanistan. I don't know anything about war, and quite frankly, I don't want to, because this war hurt him to his very soul. It took all of my time and effort, and as much love as my heart could hold to help him regain his happiness, pride and dignity. I read his every look and movement, sensed his anguish, and it pained me. I shared his hurt and misery, as I am one with him in spirit. It took me quite a while to prove my loyalty and love could soothe the beast within him. I am not good with time memory, but our story began as Rick lamented his war wounds.

It seems he's facing a desolate future. Little does he know that that idea is wrong in oh-so-many ways. I chirp and smile and my body bends in excitement. I'm awakened to the promises of what can be. When he first returned, however, he only saw a future of bleakness and desolate.

One

Corporal Richard Gonzales, USMC, stared at two magpies darting in and around the crabapple tree in his parents' front yard in south central Montana. The scene played over in his mind as if he were trying to lose himself in the freedom of these flitting birds. Solemn, almost morose, the Afghan War veteran rocked his wheelchair back and forth. Lying on the porch in front of him was his trusted Australian Shepherd, Falen. Falen was involved with a butterfly cavorting in the flowers right in front of her nose. The Aussie knew something bothered her new master, but try as she might she couldn't figure out the cause. It had been three months since the joyous welcome-home-party Sergio and Isabel had hosted for their returning son.

Javier Coronado, along with most of the ranchers in the Absoraka-Beartooth Mountain region came to welcome the hometown hero back to his family's ranch. During this celebration Rick and Falen met; it was love at first sight.

The red-headed Aussie never left the side of Rick's wheelchair and much to everyone's delight, she kept bringing him an old sock for a game of tug-of-war. The marine endeared himself to the frolicking pup by sneaking bits of his mother's food to her under the table. The bond they were forging was a match made in heaven. Falen sensed a need in Rick. While he laughed at her clowning, there remained darkness behind his eyes, eyes that had seen a lot of suffering and pain. Falen sensed his despair and depression. When Javier and Falen's mother, Jenny, had to leave the party, Falen wouldn't leave the wounded vet's side. She stayed with Rick from that night on and became his constant companion.

Falen talked to herself. This was a habit she had started since she had moved over to Rick's house and left her family, only a hilltop away, at Javier's. She had tried to talk to the Aussies that worked for Rick's father, Sergio, but they were much too serious for a flighty miss like Falen.

"I guess Master and I are the only things worth talking to," she mused.

Falen smiled to herself and rolled a little closer to the aeronautical bug flitting up and down over the crowns of the roses.

Rick positioned his wheelchair so the afternoon rays of the Montana sun didn't obscure his vision of the front yard and surrounding fields he loved. He reached to scratch an itch on the leg that wasn't there. His right leg had been left on a road in Afghanistan just about 40 clicks, or kilometers out of Garmser. As a member of the 3rd Battalion of the 1st Marine Division, Cpl. Gonzales, a battle-hardened veteran, engaged insurgents for over six brutal months in some of the heaviest fighting the Corps had seen. His squad, on a routine patrol was jolted when the right rear tire of the Humvee rolled over one of the many IED's planted along every road and path. The shock of the explosion bucked the mechanized armored truck like a wild horse, throwing Gonzales out the back and right into the middle of the blast area. The detonation was strong enough to create a fire, engulfing not only his Humvee, but also those vehicles in front and behind. Rick's right leg was mangled, but still attached. He tried to stand, but fell back almost into the fire. He couldn't block out the screams of his troopers as they tried to fight their way out of the burning, twisted wreckage. At peril and pain to himself, Gonzales limped and crawled trying to assist his wounded troops to safety. By the time the corpsmen arrived too much damage had been sustained and they couldn't save his leg. The way he reasoned, he gave a limb where many of his fellow marines had given their lives.

The afternoon shadows inched further into the front yard. Falen kept running out in the grass and bringing her Flippy back for Rick to throw. Her Flippy was a rubber Frisbee that allowed her to shake her head from side to side, banging it against her face. She loved it. He tired of this game long before she did, and when he tried to rest, she would sit by the side of the wheelchair, rubber Frisbee in her mouth and whine.

"Alright little girl, I'll toss it one more time, but then we've got to stop, OK?"

She just looked into his face knowing she had won and knew he would be throwing the floppy disk until dark.

Sergio and Isabel, Rick's parents, had gone into Billings for the day and didn't plan to be home until almost midnight. If Rick and Falen were going to eat, they would have to fend for themselves. One of the hired hands fed the working dogs and the stock, so at least Rick only had to look out for the two of them.

As he was arranging the wheelchair for a retreat into the living room, Falen raised up staring down the drive at a car pulling into the property. It was an automobile neither she nor Rick recognized. Falen assumed the strange intrusion might be a threat. Her hackles were bristling, on guard for any attack.

The Spirit of the Day and Night permeated Falen's thinking all of the time. She knew how much her mother's faith served to save Bandit and her from the freezing snowstorm that trapped them in a cave for a month. She heard many times how the Spirit guided

Bandit in the fight of his life with the criminals who tried to burn down Javier Coronado's ranch. Only Bandit and the Great Pyrenees, Gabe and Mike, managed to foil the attack and save all that Javier owned. Falen sought to be as brave as her brother in the face of trouble.

She rose up, ears alert and senses keen, leaning into her front legs facing whatever danger this strange car might bring. Rick put his hand over his eyes in a salute to block the glare by the afternoon sun, but try as he might he couldn't make out the form of the driver through the tinted windows. Small beads of sweat popped out on Rick's forehead.

He didn't expect trouble, but being in a wheelchair reminded him of how vulnerable he was. Rick hadn't met anything in his life that terrified him.

He had been afraid, especially in Afghanistan, but never too frightened to act or too scared to defend himself.

His strong hands tightened on the arms of the chair just as the black car rocked to a stop. The windows were still rolled up and the driver's door was opposite the view from the porch. Falen's barking had lowered into a persistent growl halfway between a whine and a menacing, warning sound. Rick could feel his heart beating. What would he do if this were a threat?

Two

Rick had experienced this kind of suspended animation time and again in the war zone. A threat caused his mind to slow down so his body could deal with the situation. Now here at his parents' ranch in Montana, where he never expected any danger, he was sensing the same anxiety he lived with every day for his entire tour in Afghanistan. When would these feelings stop invading his being?

"Rick" a voice called. "Ricky Gonzales, I have raced over here to see you," the effervescent conversation continued as a tanned young woman's smiling face appeared over the top of the car.

Falen glanced at the approaching figure and back to Rick in an effort to ascertain the menace. The voice carried no threat and sure enough the smell coming from that direction was delightful, but just in case the Marine needed help, Falen stood ready and willing.

"Do you like my new ride?" Five foot seven inches of all-American beauty rounded the front of the Toyota Corolla and headed straight for the porch with a smile as big as the Montana sky. Rick couldn't believe his eyes. The vision he carried with him into battle over and over, the face he dreamed of every lonely night rushed toward him in living color. Even Falen jumped back chirping a greeting and started her tail-less butt wiggle that only an Australian shepherd can manage. Dancing with pleasure on her front feet, first on one foot and then the other, Falen understood this was no person to be afraid of but instead, someone to be excited about.

"Master, it appears this human knows you, and by the expression on her beaming face she likes you very much," Falen chirped.

Falen leaned against the wheel of the chair; her almond shaped eyes darted from Rick to the young woman and back again. This had to be something to be happy about, Falen thought. She couldn't stop barking, her voice overflowing with joy.

Rick tried to cover his missing leg with the throw his mother had knitted for him. The last time he had gazed into this astonishing face he was standing on two legs and saying good-bye to her at the airport in Billings.

But now, he couldn't stand to greet her if he tried. His heart pounded. A clammy feeling in his hands caused him to wipe them on the coverlet over and over. Rick stiffened as his high school sweetheart, Susan Burton, threw her arms around his neck leaning over the wheelchair as if it didn't exist.

Falen shifted out of the way. She wondered who this person was who seemed to be hugging Rick. The woman appeared harmless and Falen's keen sense of danger wasn't ringing any alarm bells. Rick's tension rose however. He stiffened in the metal chair and held his breath while Susan caressed his shoulders with an exuberant embrace. Falen watched with fascination, while still assessing the situation.

"It's been so long. I've thought about you every minute of the day since I got the news about your condition.

Condition, Rick thought. Condition is a hell of a word to describe my life being destroyed.

Falen looked up into her master's painful face. Did she need to do something, make some sort of warning or lie down near the chair in case she sensed any danger to her beloved Rick? Maybe if she brought him her Frisbee it would cheer him up.

Three

Cold winds have a way of cropping up in Montana even on the warmest of days. Today proved no exception. Susan released her grip on Rick's neck and stood up and brushed her wrinkled blouse thinking to herself she should have said injury and not condition, worrying she had made Rick uncomfortable. A semi-smile crossed Rick's rugged face as he tried to accept this unexpected show of affection. A ringlet of brown hair fell over her left eye as she gazed into Rick's deep brown eyes.

"This is quite a surprise," he mumbled. "You look great". The awkward utterance was spoken without much self-assurance. Susan Burton on the other hand radiated confidence. She squared her shoulders and pushed the brown curl of hair out of her eyes and said, "Richard Gonzales, you have such a way with words. I swear you make a girl's heart go all aflutter." She laughed at her own joke and placed her hand on Rick's right arm with a gentle pat. He glanced down, his eyes focused on the area of his missing leg. Once again a frown clouded his face.

Susan saw the change as did Falen, who stood up, walked over and gave his left hand a good strong lick.

The dog's eyes mirrored each expression of Rick's.

Falen could sense when her master was bothered or when he drifted off into the dismal place he never let anyone share. On these occasions Falen would lie by his foot and wait for the mood to pass. Susan hadn't experienced this darkness; the Rick she remembered was always lighthearted, funny and confident. He couldn't have been the valedictorian of the senior class and hero of the football team without a whole mess of macho. Her eyes misted as she recalled the memories of their goodbyes and promises made at their last meeting at the airport. My Rick, she thought back, an American warrior, off to avenge the actions of some people from halfway around the world who had committed murders on our sacred soil. Now standing next to him, she saw only the boy she had had a crush on since the seventh grade.

Falen let out a slow whine as if to assure her master of her presence and devotion. The Aussie rested her muzzle on Rick's left hand as she nudged her body closer to his left leg.

Susan's hand dropped to stroke Falen's red head. Big almond colored eyes gazed into Susan's, grateful for any expression of kindness. Falen sensed Susan's uncertainty in what to do or say, and she sensed her love for Rick. Falen's main purpose in life was to give joy and receive it and she received it from Susan. Susan was bonding with Falen as well.

The delicate hand on Falen's head radiated warmth, warmth this young woman was eager to share with Rick.

The wounded Marine shifted his weight in the wheelchair. His nature told him to stand up, but his body wouldn't respond. He hated being a cripple.

His war wound had become a source of resentment, spoiling everything he did or thought. The exception was his love for his Aussie.

A few uncomfortable moments passed with no one speaking. Rick said, "You really look wonderful." His mind flashed, 'Is that the best I can come up with'?

Words flowed so easily between them before he had left for the Marine Corps. Since he first ran into her outside the

Junior High school the week she moved to Big Timber, it seemed the two would have lives that were intertwined. After a few awkward moments all those years ago, they fell into an easy conversation. That ease lasted for years. At this moment, however, he had little to say. A stark difference from when they had first met.

During their awkward silence, they each thought back. The school year had started and Montana was ripe with all of its celebrated fall colors. Rick walked toward school on Anderson Street kicking at fallen leaves just behind the attractive new girl, Susan Barton. In a small town like Big Timber, Rick knew all of the kids. He had gone to grammar school with all of them. A stranger stood out, and Susan Burton's stride and her brown hair bouncing on her shoulders would make her stand out in any crowd, stranger or not. Tan legs reached out in self-assured steps, just as if it were

Susan who had lived here all of her life. Rick began to whistle a pop tune to get her attention, but decided to quicken his pace to try to catch up with 'the new girl in town.'

Now as he stared into her face again, the memories of their first meeting flooded his mind making him as tongue-tied as he had appeared so long ago. Here in the present, he mumbled, "You look great." This time he added, "I really mean it."

He fought the inner urge to stand. His wound treated in Germany and later in the States had been anything but a simple amputation. The blast of the IED not only mangled the muscles in his lower right leg,

But the horrific blast had also crushed the knee and a section of his femur. The nerve damage caused such pain that fitting him for a prosthetic had to be postponed. Rick had to be driven into Bozeman twice a month for rehab to make sure the wound was healing.

When the stump became pain-free, he could he get his new leg.

The cold wind increased, blowing the brown curl back down in her face. Rick tried to hide his feelings, but his expression showed the embarrassment for being in his words, 'Half a Man.'

Falen Two

I remember how helpless I felt the day Susan visited, as she tried to get Rick to understand that he didn't have to go it alone. We, Susan and I, were surrounding him with love, yet all of that caring couldn't get him past his sense of his own abandonment and misery. Rick was his worst enemy and didn't know it.

Let's think for a minute about how I know all of this. My understanding, being a dog, is not limited to words, conversations or speeches. We animals were blessed by the Spirit of the Day and Night with good judgment of the connection to all things living. We bathe in the cool breezes, wash our souls in the warmth of the Sun, relax our minds and bodies by starlight and thank the creator for our existence. We sense changes in body chemicals long before a human recognizes that anything is going on, because we are always in tune to those around us. We are not solely focused on ourselves. We canines possess what is called a tactile nature; soft caresses and loving strokes massage our whole systems.

We use that on our humans and can often by touch change their spirit for the better. Odors most people ignore in passing are perfume to our sensitive noses. We smell fear. We smell distress. We smell uncertainty. Most important is the fact that we are concerned with just one day at a time. We don't waste our time and energy in planning for the future. I've found being a dog allows me to concentrate on the moments I am living and enjoy them and everything around me to the fullest.

When I think back to the first day Rick spent with Susan, I am saddened that he couldn't relish the gentleness of her glances and find the comfort in her touch. I noticed that her heart overflowed with love for her friend, and my instincts shouted that Susan could be the first step back from his nightmares. All the whining, smiling and pats with my paws wouldn't cajole him into seeing the devotion Susan was offering or the sting his rejection was inflicting on her willing heart.

Four

"Damn you," she shouted at the dashboard of her Corolla. Pounding the steering wheel she screamed out, "Damn! Damn! Damn!"

All the way out to the Gonzales's ranch she had fantasized about the reunion with Rick. The handsome marine was always present in her mind. Her daydreams at her desk at Fernhurst Life and Casualty in Chicago replayed in her heart as vivid as if she was reading some popular romance novel.

The Burtons moved to Big Timber because of Fernhurst. Cecil Burton had been a major executive in the southern branch of the insurance company's office in Atlanta, Georgia. The agency in Big Timber became available and Cecil jumped at the chance to buy it. He wanted to spend his life fishing and riding horses in the 'heaven' he often dreamed of in Montana. Susan grew into a Montana girl while her mother kept her deep

Southern roots alive and well. At every opportunity, LaNelle Simpson-Styles Burton would regale anyone within earshot of the importance of a proper 'up-bringing', and how blessed she had been to be from such a wealthy and important family.

Not until freshman year in college did Susan discover all of her mother's bragging and pretensions were lies. In fact Susan learned from an aunt on her father's side that LaNelle had come from a family barely above the poverty line. Her mother never knew of Susan's knowledge of her phony story, but the deceit caused a rift in their relationship. Trust is a precious thing that must be cultivated. Once the seeds of doubt are sown they take root and could become an insurmountable obstacle. Young Susan cursed her mother for driving the wedge between she and Rick. The hateful words raced through her mind as if they were spoken yesterday.

"Why, Susan Burton, how could you think of such a thing? A Burton going to the prom with an Hispanic! I declare! What would proper people think?"

LaNelle Simpson-Styles sniffed like the thought of her daughter dating beneath her status might break her heart. "This would never happen in Atlanta." LaNelle drew in a breath over her clenched teeth and the sound grated on Susan's ear.

Susan spent prom night in her room listening to the radio and crying. She never told Rick why she couldn't go to the dance with him. Rick being raised in Montana never thought of the bigotry behind the decision. He accepted the fact that she couldn't go and, while disappointed, he didn't go either.

"Damn her to hell and back." Susan wiped her eyes with a Kleenex found on the seat beside her. "Damn her and her hurtful ways."

With both hands on the steering wheel she let her anger drive the car and the speedometer reached 90 plus miles an hour. Tears flooded her eyes. Her heart pounded and the moisture on her hands made the steering wheel slippery. Over and over one sentence repeated itself.

Friendships and relationships are like spring flowers. Too much heat and they wilt; not enough sunshine and they fade. This is how it was between these high school sweethearts. Rick was busy with football and helping his father tend the cattle. Susan stayed busy trying to be the perfect daughter to a not so perfect mother. The snatches of time she and Rick spent together only led to fantasies of what might be. Their desire manifested itself in their dreams. Forbidden love is sometimes much hotter than a realized affair. Stolen glances, admiring each other from afar, and times spent in a brief span together built this crush into something they both treasured. At the Billings airport when Rick was shipping out for the Marine Corp and Susan was heading to Chicago, their meeting led to a bittersweet embrace. Promises of keeping in touch, a slight caress or a longing look seen in each other's eyes built the foundation of a long distance romance. Both wrote, e-mailed and tried to speak on the phone, but the ease they enjoyed in high school wasn't present in their grownup conversations. After Rick went to Afghanistan and Susan lost herself in work in Chicago, their missives became more and more strained.

When Rick was wounded and later convalescing in the hospital in Germany he cut off contact. Being deprived by her mother of any lasting affair, Susan had no trouble substituting work as a replacement for affairs of the heart.

Yet, the time spent with Rick moments ago brought forth a stirring in her heart she hadn't felt since she and Rick had satisfied their desires while on a Future Farmers of America trip to Billings.

Five

The screen door slammed in Falen's face as Rick wheeled back into the house. Her brown eyes clouded over as she pressed her nose into the closed door and uttered a soft whine, straining to see him, hating to be separated.

"Master, don't you want me with you? I can perform all sorts of tricks for you. I would make you smile. I need to help you through this dark time."

Falen's disappointment sent waves of sorrow through her whole body. The desire to be needed pulsed in every core of her being. She wanted to convince him she might help.

"You want to play Frisbee? Or I can just sit by your chair and offer my heart up to help calm whatever is bothering you."

Her joyous eyes faded into a dull haze. Aussies' are never happy unless they are useful.

No matter whether it's making themselves into clowns or working livestock all day in the fields. Falen had dedicated her life to protecting Rick and looking after his every desire. Again she whined and pawed the screen in an effort to get Rick's attention. He only sat in his metal chair with his head lowered and stared at the stump of his right leg.

Slowly Falen turned away from the front door and walked to the edge of the porch. She jumped to the ground and sauntered over to the crabapple tree in the middle of the drive. The afternoon breeze ruffled her coat as she stared down the lane toward where the car had passed. Falen wondered why this woman's visit brought so much sadness to Rick. The young marine didn't deserve any more hurt in his life. Falen let her body plop into the grass near the trunk of the ancient tree. Filled with doubts, she wondered what she might do to alleviate this dark mood of Rick's. She rested her beautiful head on her snowy paws and continued a soft whine of sorrow.

In the house Rick didn't even notice Falen was still outside. Clouds of embarrassment plowed through his thoughts. He hated how he had acted toward Susan. The biggest drawback to being so injured is the constant awareness of the disability and how it may possibly affect others. His relationship with Susan had never matured to a level of trust, and certainly not acceptance. Time apart seems to only postpone any chance of growth.

Many times Rick wished they were still back in the easier times of high school. As they both grew into adulthood they were separated, Rick at Montana State and Susan off in Chicago at Loyola University.

LaNelle Burton thought her girl would meet a whole different class of young men at the famous university. LaNelle couldn't wrap her mind around any chance of Susan falling in love with a local boy from Big Timber, let alone an Hispanic. Even though they phoned and emailed daily, the feeling wasn't the same as being able to see her in the halls of school. Rick, busy with studies and football, didn't have a lot of time to date, so this long distance affair appeared to be only in his mind and heart.

As proud of their son as Sergio and Isabel were, they were not a touchy-feely family. They relied on respect and loyalty to express their caring. Sergio was much better at telling friends and neighbors how proud he was of Rick; he assumed Rick somehow knew the depth of his love. Rick did know, but affection wasn't expressed in words, just deeds.

All the time spent at Montana State and then in the Corps, Rick wished he could have been more expressive about his feelings. Now the sudden arrival of Susan caused the old nervousness to manifest itself again. He had never believed himself worthy of her and now that he was crippled that old closeness seemed even more distant. With Falen outside, and Rich alone in the house, he freely let the tears flow. He buried his head in his hands and sobbed

Outside Falen stirred. Pacing the length of the porch she solemnly walked to the edge looked out into the yard and turned again to stare at the closed screen door. Something appeared to be wrong; she turned and ran to the door only to be separated from her Master by the closed screen. Inside the phone rang.

Six

By the forth ring, Rick answered the phone.

"Hello." A little apprehension in his voice; Rick wasn't expecting a call. What if something had happened to his Mother and Dad?

"Rick, this is Susan, please don't hang up."

A slight grin crossed his face, "No way, no how."

Months ago when she called the hospital in Germany, Rick couldn't handle the conversation. He thought it would be about pity, so he broke the connection. After running the chat over and over in his mind, he blamed his rudeness on pain medication. In reality her voice reminded him too much of better times and his heart balked at the recurring memories. Here was another chance, another phone call, and a different time and place.

"Ricky, I want to apologize for barging in on you this afternoon. I forgot to give you a warning. I so wanted to visit you that I just charged right over."

"No apology is necessary. I enjoyed you being here." Susan thought she detected a small amount of strain in his voice. She went on "I should've called first, but you know me, enthusiasm takes over and my manners fly out the window."

"Well, to tell the truth you surprised me pretty good," he laughed.

Since the welcome home party months ago Rick hadn't been around too many folks, especially a person he cared for. He thought to himself, "would this stress of losing his leg ever leave him?" He stared into space as silent moments passed. Rick recovered and added, "I thought you were working in Chicago, and I couldn't believe my eyes when you came bounding out of your car. By the way, what a nifty new set of wheels you got yourself, girl."

A smile crept across his troubled face for the first time in days. Susan being on the line created a warm feeling in his chest.

"Well, Mr. Rick Gonzales, you are going to have me around for quite a spell since I've moved back to Big Timber."

He gasped, searching for something to say. He pushed his left hand against the wheelchair arm and attempted to readjust his position. Falen barked and pawed the screen outside, begging to be let in. Rick said, "Can you wait a minute, Suz? I'm going to let this yapping dog back in." Wheeling himself over to open the door, Falen bounded in like a racehorse breaking from the gate, jumping up trying to get into the chair with him to lick his face all over.

"Am I hearing that adorable Aussie I saw when I was there?"

"None other. Falen visited me the night of my party and quickly took up residency." He scuffed her head. "She's one of Javier Coronado's pups out of his Jenny dog and that great Champion, Warner. Oh boy, is there a long history in that story."

Falen recognized him talking about her and nothing pleased the red-tri more. Rick laughed, and thought that if Falen had ever had a tail, she would have shaken it off by now, but being tailless like most Aussies, her butt got the full benefit of the wiggle.

Boy, was Falen happy. A grin spread across her face, her red tongue lolling out the right side of her mouth. She whined a loving sound as all the while Rick messed up the fur on her neck.

She had heard her Mother, Jenny, say many times, *"It's a shame people don't understand dog talk. There is so much we could teach them, but that's the way the Spirit of the Day and Night made it. We'll just have to continue trying to make them understand us by signs and expressions."*

"Only, if only." Jenny stopped her dissertation long enough to give a good scratch behind her copper ear, paused for a minute and looked up at Falen, and continued, *"Well, my beauty, you will learn soon enough. In dealing with the people animals, you may have your heart broken many times. No matter how hard you try to protect and serve, they will leave you and ignore you just when you could be the most helpful to them."*

31

Now almost in Rick's lap with the wheel- chair about to tip over, Falen wondered if Rick would be the type of person who would break her heart? She jumped down and Rick continued his talk with Susan.

Seven

Trying to hang up, Rick's hand slipped and the phone dropped to the floor beside his wheelchair with a bang loud enough to wake the dead. The chair almost tipped over as he reached to retrieve the portable receiver. Quickly, making sure she didn't turn Rick's chair over, Falen picked up the phone and sat down with it in her mouth in front of the smiling marine and, presented it like a trophy.

This should show him how helpful I can be. He needs me and he needs to keep me close to him."

Rick convulsed with laughter, took the phone from Falen's mouth and said, "My good looking redhead, you are something! You may be the smartest female I've ever seen. Don't you tell Mama I said that", he reached down and embraced her beautiful face. Falen's bright eyes could have lit up the room. Love never felt so good. "Old girl, let's go into the kitchen and procure us some grub. As smart as you are, I wouldn't be surprised if you wanted to cook."

Falen understood every word Rick said, and she loved the fact that he was extremely pleased with her. She knew she might find some kibble if he would want to join her in her supper.

Dinner didn't seem a hard thing to prepare. Isabel, always thinking about her family, had left a tamale casserole and a coconut pie in the fridge. Fresh milk was always in abundance at the ranch, so between the casserole, the pie, and Rick's two glasses of ice-cold milk, dinner hit the spot. Rick had warmed up some beef broth and mixed it in with the dog food, which Falen wolfed down. They both climbed into bed, no kennels for Miss Falen, and in a matter of minutes the two were out like a light.

Eight

The pressure became unbearable. No matter how hard he struggled, the marine couldn't break free from the clutch the two men had on his arm and leg. All around him, loud shrieks and sounds of torment echoed off the steel walls. White hot air seared his lungs and forced him to breath in shallow gasps. Struggling to wipe his eyes from the dust and sweat pouring down his face, he tried to pry loose the vice-like grip on his other arm. The more he fought, the tighter the hold became. All the while the screams pounded his ears. The noise grew louder and louder, making it impossible to listen to what the two men were shouting. An immense weight pushed against his back. The force on his back didn't hurt like the excruciating hurt from the contraction of his ankle. The searing pain of the grip keeping his other arm squeezed to his body. No sound escaped from his throat, no matter how hard he tried to call out. The smell of death swirled all around him. Panic rose from his stomach like hot acid. He felt this was the end.

The larger one of his captors let go of his arm and started pulling on his right leg. The muscles seemed to be shredding from the bone. They furiously worked to pull his leg from his body.

"Rick, Rick?" He couldn't tell where the voice came from, but as he tried to place it, the soothing words seemed to drive away his pain.

"Rick, Ricky." "Wake up! It's Mama. You're having a nightmare."

Falen licked all over Rick's face trying her best to wake him. Her warm breath covered him like a wet rag. She made a "murfing" sound because her heart was breaking. The thrashing and jerking around in his sleep worried her, but now her beloved master was awake and Falen pounced on him, glad that he seemed all right.

Isabel rushed over to her son's bedside gently sitting down next to him. She wiped the sweat from his forehead, saying "Mijo, mi Nino. Oh, my Ricardo. How I love you and want you to be happy. This terrible loss has affected you deeply and I so want to see your happy smile again. I pray nightly to the Virgin for your healing. Your Papa and I are so proud of you and all you've done."

Rick scooted over to the edge of the bed letting his good leg swing down to the floor. Falen moved ever so little making sure she maintained contact with her master's body. Neither the Aussie nor his mother stopped caressing Rick. He continued to breathe in short pants, but the longer he sat up the easier his breathing became.

The Afghan war vet looked into his mother's eyes and rested his hand on the top of Falen's head. The pup softened at his touch. Tears still filled Isabel's worried eyes.

"Mama, I know you love me. I know that with all my heart. And I love you just as much." He absently fingered the end of the stump where his right leg used to be.

"You and Dad have been so wonderful ever since I've been home." He chuckled, "How would I have gotten to rehab without you and your so-called driving skills?" She patted him on the cheek in a mock slap.

"There you go, sounding like your Papa again. I can drive as good as you two, better than your Papa.

"Now, Mama, don't start off on a Spanish diatribe about Dad and me never appreciating you." She reached over and massaged his hand.

"If it weren't for me, neither of you Gonzales men could do anything. You get dressed now." Isabel put on her stern matronly expression "I am cooking breakfast; Los huevos y el tocino con frijoles y tortillas calientes."

When he heard what his mother was cooking, Rick's stomach growled. It was so loud that Falen jumped back in alarm. The Aussie tilted her head first one way and then another trying to figure out where the strange sound went.

Isabel turned and left the room followed by Falen, who was sure she was going to get some table food. Rick smiled as they walked out.

The smile faded when he was again alone. He dropped his head into his trembling hands and wondered under his breath, "How long is this dark spirit going to hold me in bondage?"

Nine

No moments in Rick's young life were spent without the horrible memories of the battle of Fallujah being played and replayed in his mind. The wounds were too raw, the dreams too vibrant, the pain too overwhelming for him to be able to reach out, either mentally or physically, beyond the darkness in his soul.

Even in Germany at the airport at Ramstein when the C-17 touched down with her cargo of wounded Americans who had given so much for their country, Cpl. Gonzales gazed from face to face in the airplane seeing his fellow troopers all in pain, all afraid, and all hoping against hope the medics at Lundstuhl, the largest military medical facility in Europe, would somehow ease the pain and save their lives.

Rick tried to keep from crying. As they unloaded his stretcher at the hospital entrance a chaplain was giving the wounded, hope. Making the sign of the cross over each soldier and reassuring all of the troopers, "You are safe now. You're in Germany and you are going to be cared for."

The Catholic priest had shared those comforting words for over six hours by the time Rick's stretcher arrived. As young Gonzales peered into the eyes of the Padre, he echoed, "Amen".

Now back at his home and on his way to recovery he wrestled with the fact that he had shut Susan out when she was trying to console him and reconnect to something they both held dear.

Nearly a week after Rick's horrendous nightmare, Susan Burton called again. This time she found a much more willing conversationalist. Rick's mood brightened mostly because of Falen's never letting him get in his morose state for any length of time. The Aussie accomplished this by always playing and forcing him to pay attention to her instead of stewing in his misery.

From morning until late in the evening Falen's face appeared as if a Frisbee was growing out of her mouth. The more she played, the happier Rick seemed to be. Falen worked as hard as possible loving every minute of the time.

"Master, I will keep running and fetching, if you will only keep that happy expression on your face."

It was hard for her to talk with the plastic disc in her mouth all the time, but the expression in her big brown eyes showed Rick how pleased she was to play this game.

The ringing phone stopped the fun for a moment.

"I need somewhere to plop down. This running and running is about to kill me," she muttered. She spied a shady spot under the porch chair, which appeared mighty inviting.

The latch on the screen door was at a good height, making it easy for Rick to open and propel his chair through. As he pushed his way toward the phone the left wheel hit against the wall knocking one of his never used crutches to the floor with a loud bang. Falen jumped up, always vigilant, but soon discovered there was no danger, and her needed rest prompted the tired body back under the green chair.

"Hello Susan, yes he's right here."

Isabel passed the phone to her son and turned to go back into the kitchen. As Rick started to speak, his mother glanced back at her only child. She wiped a tiny tear from her eye; glad he was safe at home, but sorrowful that he was confined to the metal chair.

You would never have guessed that Rick seemed depressed; the lilt in his voice as he greeted Susan portrayed a bubbling personality.

"No ma'am, I don't need no insurance."

Susan chuckled, "Is that all you think of us insurance folk, always trying to sell another policy?"

"Well, I think you're always trying to sell something. What are you peddling this time? Girl Scout cookies?"

"I only wanted to know when you had to go back to Bozeman for rehab? If I drove you it would let me show off my new car to the only person in this town who would appreciate it."

Rick's mood changed. Falen sensed it and jumped on the screen door to grab his attention jumping up and down on the screen with the Frisbee in her mouth. Rick had to laugh.

What is so funny, Marine, don't you think I can drive you safely?"

"No, I'm laughing at Falen. She's nearly going crazy with her toy in her mouth begging me to come and play."

"What do you think I'm saying? I wanted you to come out and play with me."

A frown crossed his face. He paused for a second and then spoke, "I don't know. Mother usually drives me. I wouldn't want to trouble you. After all, you've got a business to run."

"Right, a business that has run itself for the last 20 years. Dad has become a human answering service. I needed a break from that phone and a ride into Bozeman will be just what the doctor ordered."

The give and take went on several more minutes and concluded with Rick saying, "Let me think about a while, if you don't mind. I don't have to be there until Friday afternoon. So, can I get back to you on this?"

The conversation went silent while Susan carefully thought out her next answer. She didn't want to be too insistent and drive him away, but she did want to encourage him into breaking the mold of his loneliness.

He had to get out of that house and into the world. She wasn't going to give up. She had been forced to give up on him in the past, and this time was going to be different.

Ten

Nothing seemed better to Cpl. Gonzales than Falen's warm body resting against his leg. He gently scratched her stomach while her eyes rolled back in pure delight. The scratching ritual had become a habit, each night before the two of them fell asleep. For the wounded Marine it soothed his psyche to be able to transfer all of his attention away from his pain and depression, and onto the soft body of his dog. Falen lived for this connection, but more than that she sensed the bonding with her master. Her legs twitched as the muscles relaxed and with each calming touch her eyelids became heavier and heavier. Soon his hand stopped as both dog and man drifted off to sleep. Rick's nighttime prayer was to keep the dream demons away. With a small whimper and a low breath from Rick they were both asleep.

The window shade remained partially opened last night when they climbed into bed and by morning the strong eastern sun shone in, filling the bedroom with a brilliant glare. Rick jumped up into the blinding light, startled from his deep sleep. He blinked as he rubbed the sleep from his eyes. The sudden movement aroused Falen and she immediately sprang up, barking at whatever intruder she felt was threatening their peace.

Outside the ranch hands were scurrying around getting ready for the early drive to the mountains. Sergio barked orders. The dogs clamored about in their kennels knowing soon they would be on their way, driving the cattle to the cool, green grazing lands high in the Absaroka mountains.

Watching the activity through the bedroom window saddened Rick. It wasn't so long ago that he would have been right in the middle of the morning's activities. A natural cowboy, his greatest pleasure was working alongside his dad. He was proud, of course, of all the accomplishments he had achieved in football, but it paled in comparison to the athletic skills needed to be a working cowboy. Now his favorite summer pastime was about to begin without him. His eyes darkened and the silent mood of sadness engulfed his soul once again.

Falen jumped up with her front paws on the windowsill and began barking at the wranglers. She was all excited and ready to go. Her memories of Javier's place and her mother, Jenny, and Bandit, Blue and the others getting ready for summer pastureland vibrated her senses.

Eleven

"Master, let's go to work. I am ready," she chirped in a voice loud enough to wake the dead. "Cows need moving and I'm the dog to do it."

She turned to glance at Rick hoping he was heading out to punch some cattle. A knock on the door grabbed her attention. "Ricardo, let's hit the kitchen table, shove some grub into our faces and see what this day is going to bring."

The sound of his father's voice broke his melancholy. He looked up, forced a smile and answered,

"I'll be right there. Give me a minute or so. Okay?"

Isabel beamed, I hope there's enough food for you two cowboys?" They both laughed at the table piled high with her usual breakfast feast. Sergio said, "I have to run outside for some last minute instructions to Hal and Tomas. Ricky, don't eat up all your mother's food." The old rancher smiled and added, "Save a little for the Don of the Ranchero"

Tomas and Hal had been working for Sergio so long they really didn't need any supervision. Sergio ran the place by himself for years, and he assumed nothing happened without him. The cowhands seemed more like uncles to Rick rather than hired hands. Rick's favorite thing about Hal was he had been on the Professional Rodeo Circuit.

After breaking nearly every bone in his body, Hal decided riding bulls in the ring wasn't going to be his chosen profession. Having been born in Southern Montana he headed back home. When Gonzales advertised in the Bozeman paper for qualified ranch hands, Hal applied. The two men hit it off and the relationship they formed had lasted for the last 25 years.

Tomas came by the ranch one day. He explained he moved to Montana from Texas looking for cattle work. His wife died in childbirth and Tomas needed a break from the dusty, dry south Texas plains. A quiet man who carried himself with dignity, Tomas and Hal formed an immediate friendship. Both men were extremely loyal to Sergio and Isabel, and to the Gonzales' ranch. Tomas lived off the main drive; Hal never married and had a small house across from the barn where "I ken keep an eye on things" he reminded anyone who would listen.

Most of the English Tomas learned he picked up from Hal. He preferred to speak to Mister Sergio in Spanish. Hal understood him, but barely, and kept saying, "You're in America now amigo, speak the native tongue." Tomas grinned and answered the old cowboy in Spanish. Sergio would laugh and laugh, and Hal just spit on the ground, shook his head and moved on.

These were the only two on earth who called Rick, "Little Ricky." Had anyone else tried there would have been hell to pay.

Falen was bi-lingual. The red Aussie barked and whined in any language. The important thing to her was that everyone at the ranch pay attention to her. She never seemed to be able to get the working Aussies to listen. She tried and tried with all of her persuasive powers, but the three working dogs treated Falen like a fluffy puppy, not good for anything other than hanging around the house.

While Sergio and Rick wolfed down the breakfast, Falen ran around outside, chirping to Hal and Tomas, in front of the kenneled dogs.

"I hope you take me with you today.

"I can work those cows heel and head", she barked loudly. She ran over to the kennels and got in the face of Roper, a blue merle, and the oldest of the group. *"You know I can help, don't you?"* She stopped for a minute and looked right into his left blue eye and continued this time in a whine, *"You know my mother, Jenny, and my brother, Bandit. I think you've tried your best to beat him in trials, but you've never done so. I am his sister and I can herd with the best of them."*

With this she turned back to Tomas. Before she continued her pleading, Sergio came out on the back porch pushing Rick's wheelchair.

"Oh, my! Where is he taking the Master? Are we going to the pasture with him? Who will push his chair? I can't! I would like to, but I'll be so busy herding cows. I can't figure out what to do. Oh, my. I so wish Bandit was here. He'd tell me what to do."

Sergio shouted at Hal over by the barn "Bring the four-wheel ATV around, will you? And, also, that big, black cinching strap with the mutton hide on the back."

Falen's head spun from one man to the other, then toward Rick and she started the cycle all over again.

"Are we going? Oh, I hope so. I will be useful again. Isn't work what Aussies are supposed to do?"

Twelve

The parade started up the mountain path. Cows bawling for their calves, working dogs nipping at the cattle's heels urging them along, Tomas and Hal on the backs of the seasoned horses and Sergio and Ricky following in the ATV. A ritual of spring repeated for as long as Sergio owned the ranch.

"This fresh air feels good," Rick said as he turned to his father. The homemade seat belt held the marine in place over the bumpy mountain road.

"This is music to my ears," he added, leaning back to let the full effect of the Montana sunshine bath his face. His right hand rubbed the red coat of Falen in her glory, perched on the back of the vehicle. The vista of the mountainside, the sharpness of the scented air, the sweet grass carpeting the way, and the constant bawling of the cows and calves, created a cacophony of pure pleasure to the dog that had been born to this occupation.

"Ah, these are the most joyful scents filling my nose. I can tell from the aroma where we are and where we are going. My heart thrills with these ancient memories."

Falen was right, deep in the collective memory of her breed dwelled the herding instinct, centered on serving her master, and helping in the movement of cattle and sheep. A purpose etched into the fiber of her DNA, and of all the herding Aussies back to the little blue dogs that first came to California. Jenny, Falen's mother, and Warner, her father, came from a long line of Aussies bred over years and years to be at a Shepherd or Cattleman's side performing this ancient dance. She sampled the air and her keen eyes darted across the landscape, trained on the cattle. Roper and the dogs dashed from one side of the herd to the other keeping everything moving in the right direction. As the lead, herding dog, Roper had years of experience in his task. The wily old veteran carried a scar on the top of his head, a visual reminder from when he was just a pup with less working experience, that he had not sufficiently ducked from the well-placed back hoof of a ticked-off mama cow irritated by his nipping her right back hock more than once, a maneuver stock dogs often use to get cattle to move forward.

Falen stood proudly in the back of the ATV overlooking the whole operation, as she thought it was her job to supervise the moving mass of black cows.

Just as Falen's mind was whirling, so was Rick's. He reached over and patted the brown worn arm of his father. He had been making this drive, usually on his own horse, since he was five years old. Being a cowboy was as much a part of the Gonzales DNA as herding was to Falen.

Rick adjusted his Montana State baseball cap to shield his eyes from the brilliant sunlight. "Dad, we've been moving these critters up to the mountain pastures for a long time."

He caressed the senior Gonzales' arm as Sergio held a tight grip on the steering wheel. The natural rocks and ravines are more of a stumbling block to vehicles than to the horses, who just gingerly step over them. The unexpected bump caused Falen to shift her weight to stay upright.

"I don't think we Aussies were meant to ride these mechanical horses. I would be much better off on the ground with my four strong legs." With the thought barely out of her mind she jumped wide leaving the vehicle and pranced alongside glancing back at Rick as if to say, *"Watch me. I'm running free and ready to help."*

Rick laughed out loud pointing at his dog, "Falen looks like she's been doing this all of her life." For the first time in a long time Rick was outside his own feelings and totally immersed in the situation on the mountain. The more Falen concentrated on the cows the more she lost track of Rick, Sergio and the ATV.

Roper seemed to have things under control. The two other dogs branched out to keep the herd from spreading out too widely and Falen scampered along joining the dance.

The cattle moved at an effortless pace up and up the Absaroka mountain pausing to sample the sweet green grass and then hurrying along at the insistence of the dogs and cowboys.

In the dusty air stirred up by all of the hooves pounding the mountain ground, Rick and Sergio lost sight of Falen. They weren't worried because she never wandered off too far and was known for her sense of direction. Rick looked over to the left of the herd in time to see her red butt headed down a deep ravine.

Thirteen

As she plunged into the crack in the mountain Falen discovered the going was going to be rough. The thick underbrush slapping her face and many of the roots clinging to the walls entangled her feet. She heard the bawling of the Angus cow and her calf as they blindly forged ahead trying to rejoin the herd, but were becoming more and more lost in the deepening gorge.

Falen's herding instincts immediately took over. She pushed deeper and deeper into the brush of the canyon trying to catch and turn the cow back toward the opening of the ravine. The cow sounded panicked. Her cries were more and more desperate, and these cries for help drove Falen on through the underbrush and debris left by the heavy currents of rushing water back during snow melts. As the winter snow melts little trickles turn into roaring streams with enough power to down trees and move logs hundreds of yards. Over thousands of years in these beautiful mountains of the Bear Tooth Absaroka mountain range, water and wind carved this rock into the beautiful panorama it shows today. The ruggedness of the terrain lends wildness to the landscape and provides a dwelling space for all creatures great and small.

"Oh my, I wish Bandit were with me. He would have the animals back safely in a minute. I so hope I can rescue them. Spirit of the Day and Night, please help me and let me be brave."

A snake warming itself on a flat rock scurried away from the fast running dog. Falen didn't wonder about other animals. Her keen mind was only on saving the cow and her calf. Sometimes the Aussie had to jump over logs that would have been easy for the cows.

Just up ahead the cow and the calf came to a stop facing a narrow opening in the ravine. Two giant rocks had slid down the steep wall sides and nearly closed the pathway, which was more of a dry creek bed than anything else. Feeling hemmed in the Mama cow stood staring at the way ahead with the calf tumbling between her legs.

"I've got to somehow get in front of them so I can turn them around before they get jammed between these rocks." The redheaded Aussie knew not to bark and frighten the animals for fear they would be startled and hurt themselves.

Two yellow eyes were watching this drama from a rock ledge just above Falen and the cattle, eager to make the calf his evening meal. A male timber wolf lay unseen from the floor of the fissure hoping for a chance to jump down and kill the calf. The lone wolf knew he was no match for the cow, but his crippled front leg wouldn't impede his kill of the young calf. Now this red dog had shown up.

The wolf weighed his chances against the sturdy dog who was nearly as big as he, and possibly in much better shape. The wolf hadn't eaten in nearly four weeks. Rib's stuck out on both sides, his hair was matted from the accident that broke his leg and left him covered in his own blood. He crawled toward the edge of the ledge trying to stay hidden. Hunger pushed him on taking over his brain at this chance to feed.

Falen caught scent of a stench in the gentle breeze cascading down the side of the gully. She gulped in air detecting the acrid aroma of the wild animal. Even though it was a new scent to her, she recognized it deep in her mind as the odor of old blood and danger.

Her eyes darted from the stranded cow and calf to the rim of the ledge trying to find out what produced such a caustic stink. She snapped back to the trouble in front of her as the cow freaked out, slashing and trashing about in a frenzy due to perceived danger. The calf bellowed and kicked back as her mother stepped on her. This scene of panic was caused by the stench of blood floating on the wind.

Falen didn't let the confusion of all of the bawling and thrashing about obscure her mission. As an Australian Shepherd she had a single mindset. Save the cattle at all cost as her breed of shepherds had done for generations.

The hunger in the wolf on the ledge and his chance for a successful kill drove him into a near rage. Yet as a hunter he lay as quietly as possible maintaining his view of the trapped cattle and the dog. The sudden sound of frantic barking from above caused him to look up startled and forget about the commotion below.

From over the rim of the gully the blue merle head of Roper appeared with fangs showing and a growl of death. The wounded wolf tried to jump up, but his broken leg caused another fall of about three feet to a small outcropping below the wider rocky ledge. The wolf was trapped between the menace of the older Aussie above and Falen, now completely trained on the sight of the predator. The wolf snarled and twisted around trying to find a defensive position.

Roper frantically pawed the ground at the top of the ravine sending small rocks and dirt down on the wolf covering his already gray coat in dust. The dirt fell into the wolf's eyes making it harder for him to concentrate on the danger from above. Falen positioned herself between the marauder on the ledge and the mama cow and her off spring. Both the cow and calf were frightened, but had no means of escape with the wolf perched on the ledge between them and the opening.

Falen jumped and leaped up the side of the canyon's wall barking her repeated warnings. The wolf's head swung like a swivel not knowing which of the dogs would strike first. The blue merle Aussie now had his feet firmly planted in the cavern wall with about half of his body leaning over the ledge. More rocks rained down on the wolf as he tried to edge into the side of a rock to protect himself.

Roper's paws lost their grip on the dirt and he plunged down onto the ledge holding the raging beast. The full force of the dog landed squarely atop the killer pushing the wolf off the ledge. He tumbled over and over until he hit the ground about two feet in front of the snarling Falen. She didn't wait to be told what to do.

Her protective instinct took over and she grabbed the wolf by his throat and pulled with all of her might. Howling with pain and covered with the old blood from his previous fracture he tried to use his legs to kick the dog and loosen her death grip. He trashed about trying to free himself and was about to succeed when the crash beside his body stunned him again. Roper had jumped to the rescue of his dog friend and his cows, and now joined in the fight. He grabbed the wolf's good front leg in his mouth and twisted as hard has he could. Falen never let go until the body of the killer went slack. She shook the body as hard as she could, turned loose of her grip and looked up to the face of Roper.

"Thank you my dear friend, we would have been goners if it was not for your protection."

She was exhausted. Roper licked her wounds and breathed confidence back into her being.

"Falen, you did yourself proud this afternoon; you saved the Master's cattle. You proved yourself worthy, and I am proud to know you and work with you. You are everything an Aussie is supposed to be."

"Hey you two, are you alright?" The worried face of Rick leaned out of the ATV peering deeper into the arroyo. His heart was beating fast as Sergio rounded the ATV and was staring down at his two dogs and the stranded calf and cow.

"Roper, move 'um" He gave a shrill whistle and repeated the command. "Roper, move them out."

The herding dog immediately sprang into action bounding off over the embedded log so as not to scare the cow and calf. He came up from the rear and gave the mama cow a low nip on her hind legs. She immediately jumped a few feet forward. Her calf followed and in no time, with the help of Falen urging them along, the dogs had the cow and calf headed back toward the entrance of the ravine, and to safety.

Fourteen

The ATV perched on the edge of the rocky ravine gave Rick and his father a bird's eye view of the Aussies and the cow and calf's progress toward safety.

"I never guessed she had so much herding in her since we've never asked her to work cattle before. It's just amazing."

"My son, you need to learn more about blood lines and how traits and intelligence is passed down from generation to generation."

"Yeah," Rick adjusted his position in the front seat and loosened the make shift seat belt to get a better view of Falen and Roper, "But doesn't it take a lot of training? The puppies don't hit the ground with that much knowledge, do they?"

The old man smiled. "I've seen babies at four or five weeks you would swear looked at ducks and chickens and wondered where they could herd them." He laughed out loud. "You should have seen Roper as a baby.

The little rascal tried his hardest to keep all of his litter mates bunched in one side of the whelping box away from his source of food and comfort, his mother. He was the boss even at four weeks."

Falen and Roper continued to push the cattle on toward the wide opening of the ravine each working behind the cows, nipping gently at their heels only when necessary, sometimes going to the head on occasion to turn a cow that appeared confused and going in the wrong direction, and other times simply giving a warning bark. Dogs who could heel low to the ground and nip a hock and then release pressure, bark a command, but not yip incessantly, those that could nip a nose forcefully, but then allow the cow to turn her head to go in the opposite direction, are the most revered as herding dogs.

Under his breath without taking his eyes off the task, Roper spoke to Falen, *"You proved yourself worthy today, little girl. I can tell that you are Bandit's sister. The same blood runs through your veins from a bountiful heart."*

If a red-faced Aussie could blush, Falen would have. Falen issued a muted thank you and stammered her appreciation in a series of tiny barks. Praise from the old veteran was sparse, and in this case Falen wanted to soak in every satisfying moment.

"You give me wonderful praise and it thrills me that a well-trained herding dog like you admires my efforts."

Roper gave a short bark like a muffled laugh, *"Falen, you are not only a good companion dog and a wonderful herder of cattle but you are also good at flattery as well."*

He gave the red-coated beauty a nip on the shoulder and raced ahead to keep the cow from dawdling along. Pleased with herself Ms. Falen nearly skipped as she ran to catch up.

Sergio kept the ATV on the top side of the ravine. Once the cow and calf had exited the canyon, the motorized horse would be used to scurry the errant cow and calf along back to the main herd.

"She is something, I've got to admit. The way she used her barks and nips to keep the cattle moving as if she'd worked cattle all of her life."

Rick grinned at the thought of his red dog's prowess. He had been around Aussies all of his life, but this redheaded mistress proved something to behold. The gleam of her coat in the open sunlight, the nimbleness of her gait, and the determination in her movement and manner brought to mind all of the great ranch dogs he'd grown up with. Thinking out loud he said, "She's better than all of them."

"Yep, she sure is, and it's no wonder knowing her family." The elder Gonzales stepped on the gas to make sure the cow didn't head back down the mountain once she was free of the tangle of the ravine. Rick noticed the area and drank in all of its beauty. At the opening of the narrow valley there were three giant trees guarding the entrance. According to the Crow Indian legends of the area, the souls of departed warriors inhabited the trees as guardians. A massive Douglas fir seemed to point to the heavens in the Montana Big Sky country. Its shadow provided a break in the vibrant sunshine. On the far side was a grove of lodgepole pine and subalpine fir with a splash of wildflowers around the trunks of each reaching out for life-giving sunrays.

As the cow and calf came to rest in the meadow Falen stopped. She stood perfectly still so as not to spook the calf. Roper came to a halt just to the east of the pair of Angus and let out a yip to keep them moving along. He did glance at how beautiful Falen was. She was bathed in sunbeams, her red coat looking electric and her chest and right leg sporting the shimmering white of her mother Jenny. She was a beauty, and all eyes were trained on her. Sergio, Rick and Roper knew it.

Fifteen

The rest of the afternoon and the climb up to the summer pastures passed uneventfully. Falen never left Roper's side, chiming in whenever she thought it seemed appropriate. Roper loved having her along and a couple of times growled at the other male herding dogs who got too close to Falen for in Roper's mind she was his and he wanted everyone within earshot to be aware. Falen pranced, as her red coat ruffled in the mountain wind. She had a constant smile on her face. Every so often she would check on where Rick happened to be to make sure of her master's safety.

As the sun half crested over the Absaroka Range, Sergio spoke to Hal and Tomas, "You boys gonna be alright up here all by your- selves?"

"Si Senor, we've got our cows to keep us warm." Both Hal and Tomas broke out laughing.

"Well, that was a mighty fine lunch you fixed Hal. I'm not sure Isabella could've done any better."

"Right!" Rick popped off. "And I am sure you want me to pass your opinion right on to her."

"Not if you value your life." All four men continued laughing. Rick placed his crutches in the back of the ATV. He swung himself in the front and buckled the makeshift seat belt. Sergio packed their things in the box in back of the seats and Falen jumped in the front floorboard ready for her ride home, and the good soft mattress she was used to sleeping on with Rick. The full moon cast a strong glow on the mountain trail that led down to the ranch.

As the vehicle bounced and lurched over the rocky trail Falen fell fast asleep. She had worked a lot harder in the past hours than catching Frisbees all-day and chasing squirrels and butterflies. She may come naturally to her herding instincts but try to tell that to her sore muscles. She whimpered each time the ATV hit a bump.

The father and son rode in silence for a long time letting the coolness of the evening breeze work its magic on their tired muscles.

"Well, my boy, what did you think of today?"

"Like old times Dad, a herd of cattle, good working dogs, and you can't beat the view."

"This land is what keeps me young, full of piss and vinegar. Since I am pushing the top half of sixty I am going to try to slow down a bit."

Talk like this bothered Rick. He had worried since the hospital in Germany what would happen if his father became disabled or too old to cowboy. How much good would a one legged cowboy be? The cloud of depression started slipping its cover again over his mind and heart.

"What are you thinking about Ricky?" "Is it something I said?"

"No Pop, just thinkin', that's all. Kinda climbed into a hole. I'm alright now, and yes, you're right, it was a great day."

A phony smile found its way across Rick's face. Although it was too dark to notice, Sergio heard it in the boy's words and tone. He quickly decided to change the subject.

"You surprised me this afternoon giving all the credit for Falen's work to her breeding. Come on, 'splain' that."

The moon glow, now fully up in the east, let Sergio relax the tight grip on the steering wheel. He reached over and patted his son's arm. With a deep sigh, he said, "We are all who we came from, son. Falen's ancestors, like most Aussies, have been working sheep and cattle for hundreds' of years. Shoot, here in America, when I was a little hombre, your grandfather taught Mr. Jim Townsend's family the art of dog breeding and care. These little rascals pushed sheep and goats all over the Pyrenees Mountains between France, Italy and Spain. I think they should have been called Basque Herders, but that is just my opinion." Sergio turned to face Rick. "The same way the dogs passed along their good points and bad, so do people."

Rick, completely absorbed in his father's conversation, reached around and rested his hand on the sleeping Falen.

Sergio continued, "Deep in our blood all of the patience, all of the strength and all of the courage we've built up over generations sustains us. Just like the red dog learns from her ancestors, so should you, my son. All of the spunk, and desire our forefathers had when they came as strangers to this land, drives you and me. Hard work, a little food and money, careful planning, and each of us made the family proud, and we will continue to do so."

A teardrop leaked out of the Marine's eyes and before he tried to answer, Sergio continued. "Look, I know how you've been hurt, and I know how you must think of yourself, as a helpless, useless half a man, but, let me assure you, your heart is full of the same guts and bravery that have been in the Gonzales' family for generations."

"We will work this out together. We will make you feel proud again, and useful again. Like your little red dog, there is a fire in your heart that will never be quenched."

The ATV bounced to a stop. Sergio pulled out his old briar pipe, packed the bowl full of Prince Albert tobacco, scratched a match on his jean leg, cradled the flame in his worn hands and sucked until the pipe glowed in the dark. The glow from the embers painted the old Rancher's face, highlighting every wrinkle and crevice etched by hard times and worry. Yet the red flame illuminated a twinkle in Sergio's eyes proving the warmth and good humor remained evident in his soul. With the pipe clinched tightly between his teeth he took his right hand and put it gently on his son's good leg. Nothing was said; nothing needed to be. The vehicle containing two men and a dog eased on down the pathway.

After dinner Rick, exhausted from the day's work fell into bed with his heroine cuddled beside him. Falen knew how tough the day had been on Rick. She 'murfed' a gentle whine, and licked his hand. Raising her glorious red head she gave the side of his face a good licking, too. Within a minute she fell fast asleep with her head resting on what remained of Rick's right leg. Softly he stroked the ruff of her neck. Yes, he thought, we are going to make this all better.

Sixteen

A breeze through his room pushed back the curtain and allowed the sunlight to pour into the window startling the sleeping marine. Rick jumped up with the sheets hanging all around him and yelled, "whose there?" afraid he was in combat again.

"Damn," the half-awake Rick exclaimed, "Somebody turn off the damned spotlight," he shielded his eyes from the glare, and patted the covers around the bed for Falen who was nowhere to be found. Some mornings Rick awoke after an especially graphic nightmare, completely disoriented. This morning was no exception; he pushed the curtains all the way back from the window near his bed.

All of the activities he watched in the barnyard made him smile as Falen pranced along at Sergio's heel hoping for some job to prove her usefulness. Her constant barks kept every animal on the place on edge.

The bulls didn't go up to the mountain pastures, and they bellowed their discontent at the red dog as if their condition was her fault. Sergio had just come from feeding the chickens, and Falen was trying her best to grab the bucket out of his hand and carry it, anything close to resembling a job.

With the other Aussies busy working the grazing cattle, Falen fashioned herself 'Boss Dog' in Roper's absence.

"You are a good doggy, my little girl."

Falen barked a cheerful chirp and nearly fell over her own feet trying to grin up at the old Rancher.

Some Aussies, when excited or nervous and especially when they are caught in the act of getting in trouble, can actually grin similarly to how we humans can. From a smile to a full-out showing of a toothy grin, can be quite endearing. It can also be disconcerting to those who don't understand this facial gesture.

"I love to assist you Mr. Sergio, you are my Master's father and we love you. Since my Ricky can't lend a hand, I will take his place."

Bouncing in front of him the Aussie nearly caused Gonzales to stumble as she, so eager to please, got her feet entangled with his.

Rick chuckled. It was so reminiscent of his childhood when being able to help with the chores was the greatest gift his father offered. Now attempting to rise up for a better view of the outside, caused him to remember how his half a leg hindered everything in his life. This morning he wasn't going to be excluded from the fun.

Throwing on his clothes and reaching for his crutches, he pushed open the back door and shouted, "Hey, wait for me, you two. Somebody has to stop all this fun and get some work done". He took the stairs two at a time on his crutches. Sergio grinned. With each of Rick's steps down the stairs the beam on the elder's face grew wider and wider. Falen looked from one Gonzales man to the other. She couldn't be more proud.

In town, it wasn't the early morning sun that stirred Susan Burton awake. She hadn't slept well, tossing and turning all night. One nagging thought was playing over and over in her mind. "Why couldn't she stop thinking of Rick Gonzales?" To her well-ordered mind she should be concerned about him as a friend, but not fantasize about what might have been, if only. If only her mother had not been such a domineering influence in her teen years. If only, she'd given into the feelings for him those long ago years. If only?

She slid her tanned legs over the side of the four-poster bed and pushed the curtain back to see what type of day was in store for Big Timber, Montana. Her mind continued its gymnastics of placing blame and trying to free herself of any guilt for life's unfulfilled promises. "Was it too late?" She repeated, "Is it too late?"

"Too late for what, dear?" came her father's voice from behind the closed door.

"Good morning Daddy, come on in. I am trying to get the sleep out of my eyes and face this day head on like an angry bull."

"I wouldn't want to get in front of that bull, girl, I've seen you with a head full of steam, and boy-oh-boy, I'd stay well clear of one of your charges". They both laughed and the warmth between them salved the worries in her mind for a moment.

"You going into the office today, or are you just going to lay around the house and live off my money?"

"I have to pick up some papers to take to Mr. Coronado about his claim from the last windstorm. He will be glad with the outcome since the company is going to reimburse his loss completely."

"Like our motto says, 'A friend in need during'

She interrupted him mid-sentence and finished singing the company jingle.

Cecil Burton thought, I am so proud to have you home again, my baby, you make the whole world right. Since LaNelle moved back to her beloved Atlanta to continue masquerading as some sort of Southern Belle, Cecil's life had much less drama. His wife burned every bridge and ruined any attempt at joy. The one person in the entire world he could count on was Susan, and now she was back at his side.

For a few minutes, it was enough. The love between father and daughter, the promise of a bright future, and the deep communication between them made words unnecessary. Yes, Susan thought, home is where I belong and Montana is my home. A bright smile burst out across her beautiful face. Behind the smile she thought, and do I love these Montana cowboys!

Seventeen

State Highway 298 weaved out as it rolled along beside the famous Boulder River. The air was crisp, the sky cloudless, and the scenery appeared to be out of a picture book. This is Montana south of Big Timber in all of its glory. Susan headed out to the Townsend Sheep and Cattle Company to give the good news of his complete insurance reimbursement to Javier Coronado for all the damage the windstorm had wreaked on his ranch. Nothing like a fat check to boost a man's spirits in this day and age. She loved calling on her father's clients, especially the old friends she had known most of her life.

Susan had the vent open on the roof of her Corolla so the clean air poured through the car. This historic valley and surrounding countryside seemed more like a movie set.

The Burtons like most of the residents in Sweet Grass County were proud their part of the world was heralded in such great movies as 'A River Runs Through It' and 'The Horse Whisperer'.

If anybody knew anything about beautiful scenery, Susan thought, it was Robert Redford. The land was as much a backdrop of life as it was for motion pictures. Susan was glad to be here out of the smoky and dirty confines of Chicago. She never got her fill of the Big Sky country.

She slowed down as Highway 298 wound through the celebrated township of McLeod. Ever since W.F McLeod moved to the valley in 1882 pushing about 125 head of cattle and 200 horses, folks have been searching out this area to plant farms and establish families. The car slowed near Holly's Road- Kill Bar and Café, as she pondered whether

to stop for an elk burger on the way out to Coronado's or on her way back home. Either way she wasn't going to miss this famous eatery. "Nope, it'll have to be on the way back," she muttered out loud. "By that time I will be a little more hungry and a lot more thirsty." A sign pointing out Natural Bridge Falls charged her memory again. A high school field trip to the famous falls was the first time she let Rick kiss her. Only a peck, but the kiss etched itself so much into her soul, that she relived the moment again all these years later. Her hands tensed on the steering wheel. Memories can be sweet and bitter at the same time.

She punched on the CD player in the car to fill the cabin with the strains of Kenny Chesney's haunting song "When I close my eyes". She blinked back the tears of how much this song related to her missed relationship with Rick. All these years later, the music had become her theme song.

Speeding along past the ranches dotting both sides of the highway, Susan let the majestic Mountains engulf her with a sense of timelessness.

This country reminded her and each person who visited here, how close to nature you were able to live. She passed a road sign for the Veterans of Foreign Wars that brought her mind back to Ricky's sacrifice in Afghanistan for the values we all take for granted here. As she sped past the entrance to the Gonzales farm, she muttered, "I might stop in on my way back."

As she passed the cutoff to West Boulder, and skirted along beside the river, she pulled into the ranch road leading to the Townsend Sheep and Cattle Company. The dust had barely settled in the parking area before Bandit jumped off the ranch house porch and ran out to greet her. Unlike Falen, he didn't bark at the first sign of her car. He never had to. His size and attitude announced before him that he was all business, friendly, but all business. The black Aussie sensed she was a friend, and politely greeted her without jumping up. His eyes were bright as can be and he uttered one bark to alert Javier they had a guest.

"Hey there Ms. Burton", Javier greeted her with a huge smile and a steaming cup of coffee. "I just made this pot fresh, can I pour you some?"

"No thanks, but a glass of water might be good."

He stopped and turned to fetch the water adding, "Come on up to the porch, Bandit will get you a seat." Susan had come to love her visits with the old rancher. Almost a throwback to the men who pioneered this part of the country, and being Basque, his knowledge of Sheep and Sheep Dogs remained invaluable to many of the recent neighbors who ranched more for a hobby than for a living.

Bandit did exactly as instructed and showed the way to the house calmly walking ahead and stopping by the guest chair. He didn't lead Susan to Javier's favorite chair, because no one but Javier ever sat there.

Jenny, Falen's mother, stuck her head out of the door checking on who was visiting. When she noticed Susan, already seated, she came over, with her butt wiggling, gave a tertiary sniff, looked up at Bandit and proceeded to lie down just in front of the visitor hoping for a complementary scratch or two behind the ears.

"How'd we do with the insurance fellas, Susan? Am I going to get anything back or are all of those fat and sassy moguls going to add my little money to their purses?" He broke himself up with his joke.

Susan grinned and opened her brief case. "Well, if that joke made you laugh then this check is going to make you hysterical". She passed the check over to the rancher.

"My goodness, girl! Where did we get all this money?" he said through the big smile, while he fingered the check over and over as if it didn't seem real.

"Well, Daddy and I twisted their arms back at the office so they would let go of some of the money they keep piled in the vault. We didn't want to have to give them a good old-fashioned Montana whuppin."

Bandit looked up as if to say, "Need me to help?"

Falen Three

Some say we dogs can understand about 162 human words. How they figured this out I haven't the foggiest idea, but there you go. Humans seem to think they know everything.

Please, I recognize we canines process more senses than can humans. I am talking about our senses being much higher than the five senses humans' brag about.

We dogs hear better and have better scenting abilities. Our ability to differentiate odors is about 500 times more effective than the capability of humans. I am so glad our first order of recognition is scent since it offers us a great cornucopia of our surroundings. It has been said if a human walks into a kitchen where stew is cooking they know its stew. We dogs in the same kitchen can detect the odors of each ingredient separately and distinctly.

Back to understanding tones of speech, facial and bodily expressions and movements.

The chemical changes in animals' bodies all speak to us dogs. Sometimes it's good and again sometimes it's bad. Our sensitive hearing coupled with a highly developed nose gives us a pretty complex view of man and beast. A human's smile can bring joy to our hearts, while a scold and harsh word could break us in two. Two of the human words I did learn to love are "Let's Go". When the master utters this sound I almost turn myself inside out with happiness. I remember the time Susan drove Rick to Bozeman for his checkup and at the last minute, Susan held the car door open for me and Rick spoke the magic words, "Let's Go."

What a day. What a wonderful trip. Susan even cracked the back window for me to inhale all of the wonderful and divergent odors that spun a tale of where we were and where we were going. The trip changed all of us in marvelous ways. I think back and believe with all of my heart that the three of us were never the same from that day forward.

Eighteen

The Montana sunshine spread through the car warming the already sunny attitudes of the three travelers.

Falen's head protruded from the open back window, eyes shut and nose gulping every pleasant scent passing on the wind. The radio blared an oldies station and Rick and Susan were playing a game of who would recognize the most songs from their high school years.

"Where in the world did the term "Doo Wop" come from?"

"You got me girl, I don't think I'm old enough to remember words like you elder people can."

"Rick Gonzales, you know I am only one month older than you are, and beside the point, you need to respect your elders."

Falen didn't care what they were saying and loved the joy filling the car like the morning sunshine. The spontaneous laugher and good humor thrilled the Aussie as much as the brisk wind in her nose.

"Listen, isn't that the Kenny Chesney song we danced to at graduation?"

Rick smiled at the memory, "Yes and the only time since your mother let you out for an evening. She would have split a gut if she thought you were with me." Rick laughed while Susan's mind flashed on the bitterness of her mother's heavy hand on her school activities.

"Hey girl, don't you go all misty-eyed on me. It's all in the past and we are now living the present."

Susan whispered "and also the future if I have my way."

The red-tri Aussie glanced Susan's way, took a quick glance at Rick, and then plunged her head back out the window.

Susan slowed the Corolla as they passed the road branching off the main highway leading to Natural Bridge Falls with all of its beauty. She still felt the tenderness of their first kiss under a huge cottonwood tree.

Breaking the momentary silence Rick added, "As soon as I get my new leg I am going to take you dancing. We'll dance to that song over and over. In fact, if I had my way, we can stop the car right now and take a turn or two, but I just might end up on my butt instead of in your arms. He grinned and looked out of the window at the land he loved so much. This reunion with Susan and the love of his dog, Falen, was the medicine the doctor must've ordered.

Nineteen

"As soon as I get my new leg… the sentence played over and over in Rick's mind. Quiet seeped into the cab to fill the vacuum when the joyous laughter fled. Susan gazed out the window, staring at the countryside she loved. It rekindled her childhood memories. Falen, tired of the wind up her nose, stretched out across the rear seat for little nap bathed in the soothing sunshine.

My new leg… his mind was a jumble trying to figure out what difference a piece of steel and wires might make in his life. He murmured, "I'll still be a cripple, always a cripple."

Completely different strains of thoughts were bouncing in Susan's head. She wanted to reach over and grasp Rick's hand. She wanted a closeness that had yet to show itself. These dark moods needed to pass and never come back. She celebrated the good times, but feared the darkness that came over her hero like an evil blanket of doom.

Falen shifted her position, never completely waking up, but straightening out her right leg so she had a better chance of catching up to the wayward calf romping in her dreams.

The Corolla rolled on up US 90 toward Bozeman. The radio was still playing, but no one was listened. The sky was as blue as the Chamber of Commerce promised, and the air was light and full of the smells of Montana's outdoors.

As the trio neared Bozeman, Falen stirred in the back seeming to realize they were getting closer. In reality though, she probably needed to go potty since she'd not been out during the whole trip. A soft whine and anxious eyes told her story.

They merged right onto 191, which is East Main Street, journeyed through traffic west to North Wilson Ave, turned right up several blocks to the VA Medical Center, and fortunately, a parking space under a tree was vacant across the parking lot near the main entrance.

Rick never wanted to be let off in front where it was an easier walk. He wanted to tough it out Marine Corps style, Susan teased.

He reached around back and fastened the leash to Falen's collar. Her entire body vibrated and her eyes shown like diamonds.

Before Susan could get around the front of the car, with Falen in tow, Rick climbed out, adjusted his crutches and fitted his USMC baseball cap to keep the sun out of his eyes.

As he leaned against the right side of the car for balance, Susan placed herself and Falen in front of him so he couldn't leave.

"Before you go in Mister Rick, we are a few minutes early and I have something to say."

Rick let his arms rest on the pads of the crutches as the morning sun shone on his face like a photographer's lights.

"Yes ma'am", he grinned with a mock salute, "I am all ears"

Falen sensed the seriousness of the moment and sat down leaning on Susan's left leg.

There was a pause. Both gazed into the other's face probing the moment. Rick almost opened his mouth to say something but thought better of it and just smiled.

Susan took a deep breath. The nerves in her stomach jiggled around and a small bead of perspiration crept its way onto her upper lip.

Another deep sigh and she started, carefully and deliberately. She began to unwind all of the emotions that had been bottled up for weeks.

The first words came out fast and furious in front of a torrent of tears.

"Rick Gonzales, I've known you for half of my life and have grown up admiring everything you stand for. Even when we were kids I kept a special place in my heart for you, in school, in town, at your sports events, almost everywhere you went.

I never thought you noticed, but always hoped in some way you were thinking of me, too."

She wiped her nose with the back of her free hand, grabbed a tighter rein on Falen, who wasn't going anywhere. The Aussie looked from one of her humans to the other.

Tears now freely flowed down Susan's cheeks as she continued. Rick again started to speak, but fortunately his brain told him to shut up.

"I can still remember the tenderness in your heart the first time we kissed at the falls. Each night as I go to sleep, I remember your touch and the warmth of your arms around me. Never in my life have I wanted another man or felt I could give myself to another. No Sir! It was going to be Rick Gonzales or nobody."

His mind flashed to the way he treated her the day she called the hospital in Germany all because of his stupid pride. His bottom lip quivered a little, which he tried to hide.

"My mother didn't recognize at the time, but her despicable nature forged my great admiration for you. I cheered for you in high school as you led the football team to victory. I cheered your exploits at the Montana State High School Rodeo. In fact, Mr. Marine, you might say I've been your number one fan for all these years." She wiped the copious tears from her eyes, and without missing a beat said, "Without you even knowing I flew back from Chicago just to see you play for Montana State."

"I jumped at the offer from my Dad to return to Big Timber after I heard you were coming home. The lapse between seeing you off at the airport and driving up your drive way was filled with millions of hopes that we might rekindle our friendship."

"Now Mr. Smarty Pants, my fire has been reignited and I am not going to let you or anyone else extinguish it. Whether or not you let me, Cowboy, I am on this ride to stay."

A long moment passed. With tears gently running down her face, she blurted out, "I love you, Rick Gonzales. I love you and Falen and everything about you both." She wiped her eyes again and said with defiance, "And that is what I have to say!"

Rick raised himself off the side of the car and reached out for her cheek. He didn't know whether to speak or keep his mouth shut. He slowly caressed the curve of her face and whispered, "Me too, you."

He took his steps toward the front entrance of the clinic, not looking back until he got to the automatic doors. But he did turn back to gaze at his girls and then he shouted "Hoorah! and turned to go into the clinic.

Falen jumped up and barked at the closing doors. She sensed something wonderful had just happened. Susan's whole demeanor softened, and the gentle wind across the parking lot seemed to be caressing them both with loving touches.

Twenty

"Excuse me, but you must be Susan, right?" Falen jumped up with a chirp and moved between Susan and the young man dressed in hospital scrubs.

"Ah, yes." Susan put her coffee down on the bench and stood up with a firm hold on Falen's leash. Worrying immediately about Rick.

"Well your ears must've been burning, because Corporal Gonzales and I have talking about you both. And let me add that you're both every bit as beautiful as he described.

Susan laughed a little as she looked down at Falen, then said "Well thank you."

Walt held his hand very still so Falen could smell him. As dogs do, she sensed his positive energy and not only sniffed his hand, but she gave him a good lick too which didn't go unnoticed by Susan.

"Please sit back down. I just wanted to quickly introduce myself.. m'name's Walt Miller, and I'm one of the PTs here at the Clinic. In my spare time, I'm also a dog trainer. So when the Corporal told me you two were waiting on him outside, I had to run out and meet you since he couldn't say enough about you.

Susan perked up, immediately understanding his kind of instant connection with Falen.

"What kind? I mean what dogs do you train and for what?" The fresh breeze blew a tuft of hair down over her eyes. She brushed it back and sat back down on the bench.

"I got out of the Army a few months ago, if you ever get out of the Army that is," he chuckled. "Anyway, in Afghanistan I worked with WMD's or Working Military Dogs as a trainer and handler. My own dog, Sarge, was named Sergeant Grit, because he acted like a hardened old top sergeant."

Falen was totally comfortable with the tone of his voice and the gentle stroke of his hand on the top of her head.

Susan was fascinated with Falen's acceptance of this man. Her time spent with Falen gave her a completely different opinion of a dog's intelligence.

"The U.S. Military is currently working with animal-assisted interventions for the rehabilitation of our wounded service men and women. It's truly amazing what these dogs can do."

"Falen looked up at Walt with an Aussie grin on her face as if to say, *"You betcha, fella! We can do marvelous things"*

Susan listened as Walt went on about the abilities of interaction between dog and man. He shared a couple of stories about Sarge and how much he missed their daily work and play since the old soldier had passed away recently. Sarge had seen a lot more of tragedy than most people.

Walt paused for a moment while the lump cleared in his throat, swallowed hard, and continued, "I think I could help you guys shape Falen up into a licensed Service dog. It would be fun for me and give the three of you something to work on together. What do you say?"

Falen was the first to respond with her tailless wiggle, and ever the cautious one, Susan said, "Let me talk this over with Rick and see what he says. Does he have your phone number?"

As he rose, he assured her that he would pass a card along to Rick inside and told her how nice it was to meet her.

Stooping down he ruffled the red headed girl's top locks and said, "I hope to get to know you a lot better, too."

Twenty-One

"You're going to school, Falen," A sudden gust of wind whipped through the trees near the park bench sending Susan's hair in several directions. She dropped Falen's leash and tried in vain to smooth her fly-away locks. Falen just stood looking up in amazement at all of the furious motion and wondered what she was supposed to do.

"I love the wind in my hair, and I don't care whether or not my coat gets mussed up. The cool wind across my face and back reminds me of running free in the mountains."

A flurry of leaves and pieces of loose paper skipped across the yard as the wind got gustier. With her hands plastered to her head she glanced up as Rick rounded the corner and headed straight for them. She quickly forgot about her messed up hairstyle as her eyes locked on the face she'd come to love. He had a different cadence in his movement. The crutches swung smoothly as he hurried across the parking lot.

As he neared, Falen gave her usual welcome bark, and Susan shouted out, "What did you do in side, throw down a couple of martinis?

I haven't seen a smile as broad since you won the State Football Championship."

"We've got a lot to talk about", he bent down with the crutches loose under his arms, and patted the red head of Falen. "Hey, girl, did you take good care of Susan?" When he looked up into Susan's face she noticed his eyes were glistening, and his smile seemed to grow even bigger. They piled into Susan's car. Rick reached back to rub his Aussie's head while Susan tried to see the street through tear-filled eyes.

Peace needs no words. The peace passing among the trio as they started back down North Wilson needed no explanation. Susan's hands rested lightly on the steering wheel, a few dried teardrops remained on her cheek. Rick kept up his drumming fingers at a steady clip. Falen gazed out of the back window and followed the flight of several birds circling in the sky. If asked, all three would have replied that this was one of the most wonderful days they could remember.

"Well, tell me all of the news. What did the Doctor say to make you so happy."

"I, uh, I mean there is so much to tell, I don't know where to start." He ceased his finger drumming on the dash and said to Susan. "I haven't been in this good a mood in a long time." She nodded. "There have been so many dark times, so much depression and fear, I have to take a breath to realize this is the start of my new life." He let his left hand caress her forearm.

Falen cocked her head, sat up straight in the middle of the back seat so she'd have a clear vision of the two people she was responsible for. The joy of life seemed to fill the car and Falen let it wash her soul. Her people were happy and happiness was her greatest basis of satisfaction. She didn't even mind that she needed to go potty so bad it was making her sick at her stomach. With a little whine Rick got the message. "Susan, let's pull over at the rest stop coming up. This puppy's bladder must be about to burst."

A misty rain begin blurring the windshield as the Corolla turned off of Interstate 90 at exit 305 and merged into the traffic on East Valley Center Drive, headed for the rest stop located at the Montana State Department of Transportation. It's a large rest area with restrooms and a picnic area before drivers climb back on 90 headed east. Folks with newspapers and coats thrown over their heads to keep off the heavy raindrops scurried toward the building housing the rest rooms. Susan spied a parking space near a grassy area that had a small overhang covering a picnic table and barbecue pit. "That's a pretty tight fit"

"I can make it. I've had this Toyota in smaller spaces than this." She looked out the side window at her mirror to make sure that she wasn't too close to an old Ford pickup on her left, she knew she had plenty of room on the right next to a small RV with stickers from all over the country plastered on the back. Once the car settled and she put the gear into park, Rick laughed, "Now how in the hell are you going to worm your- self out of that door without getting all of the mud on that pick up all over you and Falen?"

"Don't you worry your pretty little head, Cpl. You are talking to one nifty gal who specializes in tight spots."

Twenty-Two

The dashboard of the F-150 was plastered with protest stickers and decals that screamed about the abuse and danger of the American Government. Every militia group and Government protest group seemed to be represented. The driver sat behind the wheel with the window cracked to let the swirl of pot smoke drifting hazily into the air. The passenger was outfitted in camouflage with a "Live Free or Die" patch on his shoulder, which was threadbare and missing quite a few stitches on the upper arm. The floor of the cab was littered with fast food wrappers. The ashtray overflowed with butts and trash. Under the passenger's feet lay six or seven empty beer bottles with enough mud on them to signify the length of time the bottles had been undisturbed. The only thing heard from the rider in the rear seat was snores pushed by a volume of bad breath. As the rain lessened to an occasional drip the occupants seemed ready to disembark and head for the public restrooms.

"Muscles don't get your purty hairdo all wet in that storm out there." Weiner broke up. He laughed so hard spittle in his throat caused him to choke and nearly vomit. Weiner's eyes were red sockets of bloodshot. He and his friend, Muscles, the driver, and the hitchhiker they had picked up outside of Helena, had made it this far without wiping out on the freeway or getting shot for stealing from the service stations and truck stops on the interstate.

"God damn," Muscles grunted as his left foot kicked an empty wine bottle out of the door. It banged on the concrete and burst into pieces. "God damn! I sure hope we don't back over that shit pulling out. I sure as hell don't want to be fixin' a flat in this weather."

"Holy crap", Weiner said looking out of the right side of the windshield as a beautiful young woman exited her vehicle with a red dog in tow.

"What?" Muscles jumped up. "Shit, she's a major league 10, ain't she boys?"

"Dude, if it were nighttime I would make her number one on my lovin' parade."

"Oh yeah, you would, right after me." He gave pieces of the broken wine bottle a kick under the car parked next to his.

A wind gust pushed the door against Muscle's leg. Weiner wiped the vapor from the windshield to get a better look. The hitchhiker in the back seat never woke up.

Falen's leash wound around Susan's leg as the pup tried to pull away so she could find a smelly place to pee.

"Just a minute girl or we're both going to fall down," She laughed and wiped the rainwater from her eyes.

Wiping the fog from his windshield to get a better look at Susan and Falen, Rick noticed the grubby characters next to him in the filthy pickup climbing out. The man who got out on the driver's side was having a tough time standing, Rick guessed due to the amount of alcohol he'd probably consumed. If he wasn't drunk he was giving a good imitation of it. Rick got his crutches and opened his car door to stand up in case Susan and Falen needed him. He had his Marine Corps field jacket on and pushed up the collar to keep the rain from pouring down his back. His Marine issue pant was bloused on the left side and pinned up on the right. His arms, still holding the crutches effortlessly vaulted him from the cab to the pavement. He pulled the crutches under his arms and headed to the spot where Susan seemed transfixed, trying to ignore the approach of the grubby looking men.

Twenty-Three

Falen strained at the leash, her fiery eyes never leaving the two men who were now approaching Susan. All of a sudden Weiner and Muscles stopped and glared at Rick, who was working his way toward Susan and Falen on crutches. The rain continued at a furious pace, the wind's gust pushed everything in the area in waves making it hard for Rick to keep his balance.

"Hey, hero," Weiner yelled his hands cupped around his mouth. "Did ya leave your right leg in the car? You'd better run back and fetch it if'n you're gonna save this here damsel in distress."

Muscle's slapped the shorter man on the back and both collapsed in gales of laughter. Neither moved any closer to either Rick, or Susan and Falen. Yet the insults continued peppering like the rain.

"I bet you got your leg hurt when you tripped over a desk drawer, 'cause you sure don't seem like no war hero to me."

Weiner added, "Shit yeah, if you're what's protecting America it's no damn wonder we're in such a pile a shit." The camo clothing that both of the agitators wore stuck to them like wallpaper.

Rick's inner warrior was chugging on overtime. He knew just how to handle tormentors like these. They were no different than the Afghans who spoke English and shouted to intimidate the troops with constant taunts.

He needed to get closer to Susan and his dog without starting a physical confrontation with these drunks. Yet his blood boiled. Even on one leg he thought he could take them both out if he had to.

"Hobble your butt on over there by your girlfriend, 'crip'. If we wanted to we'd grab her butt, and make you watch."

Falen's attitude changed with the confusion and the screaming voices. She lowered her head and began a deep guttural growl like an attacking wolf. Her eyes blazed with anger, the hair on the back of her neck stood erect, her ears were pasted to the side of her head. She leaned ever so slightly up on her toes making sure she was between Susan, Rick and the danger.

As Susan tried to change hands holding the leash, the wet leather slipped out of her grasp and Falen was loose. The Aussie charged in the direction of the threat with a maniacal series of barks and growls. About five feet from the pair, they turned and ran for the truck. Falen grabbed the pant leg of the passenger as the driver, Muscles, rounded the truck's front fender and jumped in the open door. Weiner kicked back at Falen.

That gave her a chance to re-bite and clamp down on the lower leg. The dog twisted her head left and right viciously with the man's leg firmly in place. Weiner screamed and slapped at the Aussie's head. Rick yelled, "Falen release, release right now." She almost spit out the man's leg as if it tasted bad. She backed up still barking angrily, keeping her eyes on the backside of the man as he scrambled into the truck. Muscles kept shouting curses and obscenities at Rick and Susan, but clearly didn't want anything to do with the mad dog as he called her.

Susan ran forward to grab the leash, careful not to get within reach of the truck. Falen didn't move from the spot. Her head remained lowered, ears back and the menacing growl didn't stop.

"You'll see us again I guaran-damn-tee ya, you phony bastard. You'll hear from us again." Muscles slammed the gear in reverse. The slick tires slipped in the muddy surface. The truck fishtailed out of the parking space. "We'll teach you, American hero, not to mess with true patriots, and we'll get you when you don't have that damn dog to lean on."

Soaking wet and a little stressed, Rick stood by Falen, gently patting her head and stroking her neck. "Good girl, Falen, good girl. He and Susan continued to stroke her back and shoulders, all the time praising her for her courage. Falen's eyes became soft again as she looked up into the faces she adored.

"I wish Bandit could have seen me. I know he would be proud. Yes sir, we are a couple of brave Aussies! Yes sir!

Twenty-Four

It was almost as wet in the car as outside.

"The Sport" for lunch has to wait", Rick said as he wiped the rainwater from his face. Falen did the doggie shake spraying water all over the seat and a lot on Susan's back. The mention of lunch at their favorite restaurant were the first words either had spoken since the traumatic encounter at the rest stop. Falen sensed the tense atmosphere and did her best to remain quiet. She was still in shock. The outburst of anger proved as tiring as a hard cattle run. Her eyes retained their shine, but her wet ears still lay flat against the sides of her head.

"How are you?" Rick spoke gently and reached over to touch her right arm. Susan smiled, "I've been better" she grinned, "That whole frightening experience wore me out. I am so proud of Falen and you for diverting the danger. I've always thought that I'm pretty self-reliant, but under those circumstances I almost fell to pieces."

Falen let out a small whine in agreement.

"I only hoped I could help and defend us if necessary. Loud mouths like those two usually are more vicious with their mouths than their action."

Rick thought a moment, "But I admit, I'm glad Falen frightened them off."

A large smile broke across the marine's face, "I have some news that's not so threatening unless you're a person who is afraid of dancing."

Susan's eyes brightened. She glanced toward Rick holding her breath.

"I didn't get a chance to tell you. Really, I was waiting until we reached The Sport for lunch, but since we'll be missing my planned celebration I'll tell you now. In about two weeks we can go out on the town."

Susan started to chime in but decided better to let him continue.

"I had my final exam this morning for the prosthetic leg. The folks at the VA tell me I will be fitted and start physical therapy in about week, and before you know it, I'll stroll around, as I like to say, on my own two legs, even if one is mechanical."

"Oh, Mister Gonzales, that makes me so happy," With her left hand she tried to wipe the tears from her eyes.

Falen sensed the mood change and let out her happy bark, which is more like a chirp. She loved the sound of her own voice, so she continued. Rick reached over and turned on the radio. The sound of music played well with Falen's melodious voice.

The horrible event back at the rest stop was all but forgotten. Susan reached over and held Rick's left hand, with a gentle squeeze.

Some 30 or so miles ahead a red F 150 sped along with Muscles and Weiner discussing how to get even with those two.

Twenty-Five

The Red truck faded from Rick and Susan's concerns. Occupied by other more important thoughts, days flew by and the appointed day for the wounded warrior to walk upright again had finally arrived.

Susan again held the leash for Falen and waited like Rick had asked, outside the entrance to the VA in Bozeman. The breeze cooled the air on this sunlit day and the leaves on the trees around the parking lot seemed to be singing with the emotions Falen and Susan enjoyed. Slowly the electric doors pried themselves open and the handsome Marine, after weeks of physical therapy, walked out into the sunshine standing tall and erect. For this occasion he wore his Marine Corp dress blues. He sharply marched across the pavement with his eyes glued on the two girls in his life who had become the reason his heartbeat.

Susan beamed, her heart overflowing with the love she had been denied all those years ago by her mother's prejudice. Here walking toward her came the man for whom she'd always dreamed. The only one she ever loved.

And now that love was returned.

"Attend Hut" her hand went to her eyebrow in a salute. Rick returned the salute with "All present and accounted for."

Falen's butt nearly lost control as she wiggled faster and faster. "Cpl. Richard Gonzales, USMC, ready for duty and assignment"

"How about we invade Livingston and set up a lunch camp at The Sport?"

"Sounds like a plan to me, but you'll have to drive. I haven't got that part of this prosthetic legs business down quite yet."

Falen wasn't sure what all of this talk meant for her, but she reasoned it just might have something to do with her being left in the backseat for a while.

"With all of this sunshine I will take a much needed nap."

They found a parking space right in front of the restaurant on South Main. At lunch time the place overflowed with customers. Most were coming in for their famous burger.

"Best burger not only in the state, but in the country I'll bet!" Rick nearly leaped out of the car. He put most of his weight on the left leg, not ready to trust the new artificial leg just yet. But once he stood erect he walked as steadily as a Marine marching in review.

The cool air allowed them to leave Falen with two windows rolled half way down. True to her prediction, she fell fast asleep before her humans reached the front door.

"Hey there, Corporal, welcome back." The manager continued to welcome them as they walked down by the beautiful bar. Deep forest hues and wooden tables and chairs made this café a well know tradition since 1909. The variety of items on the menu made each meal special and different. Rick always ordered the same thing, the Sport burger, cooked on the classic flat grill, served on a Montana Wheat Parmesan bun piled high with lettuce, tomato, onions and pickles. Aside from his mother's cooking, this was the one meal he longed for when he was in Afghanistan.

Susan perused the menu and settled on the Ram, a classic gyro with grilled lamb and tzatzike sauce. Iced tea all around and the diners settled back to glory in this day of days.

"I've never felt so good in a long time. Standing without the crutches and not wheelchair bound does a lot for a man's ego."

She smiled. She was so proud of him and so thankful for the opportunity to be a part of his life. Susan was afraid to speak for fear she would melt into tears.

They didn't linger after their meal. They said their goodbyes to the staff, and headed back for the drive home. What a homecoming it was going to be, with Sergio, Isabelle along with Tomas and Hal, not to leave out ole Roper. Even Javier Coronado was going to be at the house along with Jenny and Bandit.

So fitting for this occasion, there wasn't a cloud in the big sky; just the canopy of Montana's great trees.

Falen sensed the nearness of home and began to whine her eagerness to return. She stood in the backseat with her head between Susan in the driver's seat and Rick. The trio didn't need any music from the radio to enhance their spirits. This was the day the Lord had made, and they were rejoicing in it.

Falen Four

I couldn't believe my eyes and ears as I jumped down from the car. Bandit rushed to greet me with Jenny, our mom, close behind. All of the humans crowded around Rick and Susan, while the important beings, I mean my fellow dogs, couldn't get enough sniffing, licking and covering me with their love. Bandit was the first in the line of canines.

"Falen, my sister, I am so proud of you and your job of taking such good care of your humans." His black butt end wiggled with such enthusiasm he nearly knocked our mother, Jenny, over.

"Yes my dear, your brother is right! You pups make me so proud."

Rick stood tall and erect receiving all of the well wishes from his family and friends. I did, too, since my family of dogs were doing the same for me. I couldn't wait to tell Bandit and Roper about the dangers at the highway rest stop and the angry and drunk pair I had to run off.

The party went on until nearly sunset and while the humans moved into the house for food and fellowship, we were allowed to run and play outside. We acted like puppies and couldn't get our fill of Doggie Doings.

We paused to remember and thank the Spirit of the Day and Night for our lives, our work and the wonderful masters who loved and protected us. Bandit mentioned how our protective nature had warned and sheltered all of those in our family circle. People, sheep, cows and the property we've lived on.

As I think back to that amazing day I had no idea of the trouble ahead for Rick, Susan and me. If only we could have stayed in that happy time, but we had to move on to face the darkness in store for us.

Twenty-Six

In nearly six weeks the entire area would focus on the world famous Livingston 4th of July Rodeo and Parade. Rick felt proud that he would be able to stand on his own two feet for the festivities. He looked forward to dancing with Susan at some of the outstanding "watering holes". Every day he got stronger with the use of the prosthetic leg, which added to his accomplishments of returning to a normal life style.

The wounded marine became more and more a Montana cowboy. His dad, Sergio, beamed with pride when Rick and Falen started carrying their load of the work with the cattle. Under the tutelage of the old experienced herding dog Roper, Falen learned the tricks of the trade and became more and more useful around the corrals and barn. Rick resumed riding his Quarter horse named Warrior. The gelding was about six years old and so steady Rick felt absolutely secure in the saddle. In a matter of days he imagined himself riding in the rodeo again. When he brought up the subject one night at dinner, Isabella threw down the law,

"No way, no how was that going to happen."

"A short time ago I got you back in one piece, and you think I'm going to let you do some stupid thing like rodeo riding again, you must be pretty loco, man."

Sergio laughed. He knew not to comment.

Nothing made Rick more proud or more thankful for the new life his new leg offered. He had purpose again.

Hal and Tomas loved the help and encouraged Rick, but at the same time kept a watchful eye.

Falen loved the change as well; outside with real work to do instead of just chasing the flippy all day, and trying to keep her soldier occupied.

The new busy lifestyle of Rick allowed Susan to spend more time at Burton Insurance Agency and open a new branch office in Livingston. There weren't many nights that she didn't either drop in or have him meet her after hours for dinner or just some quality time getting to know each other better. The better they got acquainted the more the affection grew. The good thing was Rick took Falen everywhere with him and when he couldn't take her in somewhere she curled up in the front seat of his Sequoia and went to sleep.

One of the rare evenings he spent at home the phone rang, but it wasn't Susan.

"Rick Gonzales?"

"Yes."

"This is Walt Miller from the VA in Bozeman. I wanted to check up on you and see if everything is working out for you."

"You betcha!" Rick ran his hand down his right thigh. "Never better!"

"Wonderful, Corporal. That's what we like to hear. I'm also calling about your Aussie, Falen?"

"That's my red head."

"I explained to your girlfriend, Susan, about our conversation at the Clinic. How dogs are being used for rehabilitative purposes, helping soldiers return to a productive civilian life. Well, I wanted to talk to you more about my volunteer work with what I think is an amazing organization called "Palz with Pawz." They specialize in training canines to serve service women and men like yourself. You see, everything you told me about Falen when we met, and my observations of her when I met her and Susan outside the clinic, well, I think she could be an ideal candidate for training. I'd love the chance to work with you two, if you're up for it?"

"Wow! Well, I am working more and more around the ranch helping my Dad, and Falen's working alongside me. She's sure been a quick study when it comes to a herding dog's job. I'd love the chance to see what else she can do. One of my favorite things about her is her intelligence and her willingness to learn and perform."

"That is the mark of a great dog. But know that her willingness to learn and perform has a lot to do with your connection. I just want to help you both cultivate that connection even further. So, if you're game, I can drop by your ranch next Thursday after I'm done with my shift. We can start slow and not put too much pressure on her."

Rick laughed, "Pressure on her? Ha! I don't think that'll be a problem!"

Twenty-Seven

Susan called to say she was to going into Bozeman to shop for a new outfit to dazzle him on the 4th of July weekend.

"Works for me," Rick said rubbing the top of his dog's head, "Falen and I are busy getting ready for this afternoon's appointment with Walt Miller, remember him? He was my PT at the VA Clinic and he's also a dog trainer" He rubbed Falen's scruffy neck, "Falen's got her work cut out for her today! I'm kind of excited."

She glanced up at Rick as if to say, "Oh Really?"

Susan said, "Well have fun you two! I'll call you when I get back."

The Aussie eyed the car pulling into the driveway, leaning forward on her front legs at full attention. Walt stopped his car and got out. And to Rick's surprise she started to chirp and wiggle.

With a smile on his face Walt greeted Falen first, offering his hand for another sniff. Now that his hand was wet with happy licks, he chuckled and said, "Yeah, hey girl, what a good happy girl you are!"

After wiping his hand on his jeans, Walt turned to Rick and grasped his outstretched hand. "Hey, trooper, it's good to see you again."

With a chuckle in his voice, Rick said "Welcome to the Gonzales ranch. We've been looking forward to this afternoon. As you suggested, I didn't demand too much of her this morning. We kept things calm and cool, which is kind of a chore with Falen." Both of the men were laughing now as they headed toward the front porch, Rick quietly proud of his new found ability to stand and walk.

"I looked into your group, 'Palz with Pawz.' I am really impressed and intrigued."

"I know! I got hooked like that when I found about PWP too. These dogs are capable of so much, it's just awesome. Many tasks require cognitive decisions. Dogs are able to sense oncoming seizures, warn of potential fires and other mechanical failures. Most important, is their ability to assist in the recovery of individuals suffering from PTSD or TBI by optimizing social support and minimize anxiety and stress."

Reaching down to stroke the neck of his beloved Aussie, Rick said, "Believe me, I know about that. I couldn't make it without this pup's contagious enthusiasm and unconditional love."

Falen peered into her master's face. Her intense eyes spoke louder than words. She loved him and would lay down her life for him.

For the next two hours Walt showed Rick training methods to help Falen learn without confusing her, and dampening her willingness to please. The trainer introduced them to the 'perform and reward system', which allowed Falen to play a game for completing a task.

"When I was 'in country' with our Working Military Dogs, my dog, Sgt. Grit, knew I had his yellow tennis ball with me at all times. As soon as he performed his task, no matter whether he was sniffing out IEDs or taking down a combatant, I was going to let him play for a while. His eyes changed as well as his entire disposition once he saw his toy.

Rick wondered aloud if he would have to haul her Frisbee around all the time. Walt laughed and said, "Nope, we will transfer her attention to a small ball, easy to carry and have with you. Falen understood all of this human talk and thought, *"I don't care what I play with as long as I get to play."*

Twenty-Eight

"Can ya tell what them two are doing?" Weiner passed the binoculars to Muscles, "I think they're just standing around watching the damned dog. And it looks like that marine is standing on two legs; damned if I know how."

Their red truck was parked across the highway from the Gonzales Ranch pasture, where Walt was working Falen. Some cottonwood trees on the opposite side of the road obscured the occupants from view. From Rick's and Walt's position they hadn't even noticed the truck that parked about 30 minutes ago, right after Walt drove in.

"Is the marine standing up?" Weiner ask. "Seems like it," Muscles said, "but for the life of me I can't figure out what the other guy is doing. This sure ain't no time to hassle them two and the damned dog."

Falen's nose searched the wind for the offensive odor she detected. It was a familiar scent, but without more trace in the wind she had a problem trying to locate its origin.

Rick and Walt continued talking about dog behavior but not noticing Falen's growing defensive nature. The more she sucked in air through her sensitive nose, the more agitated she became. She wouldn't take her eyes off of the strand of trees by the roadside. Walt let Falen's leash fall to the ground. On wolf like paws she crept closer to the edge of the pasture and away from Rick and Walt. The hairs on the scuff of her white neck stood up and her brilliant red ears perked forward to funnel in any unknown sound. The breeze through the cottonwoods rose in intensity giving her a nose full of the offending odor.

Down deep in her chest a growl rose into an ominous threat. Her warning came so suddenly both Walt and Rick were caught by surprise. The men immediately stopped talking and stared at the Aussie. Falen was a good ten yards away and moving closer to the edge of the field. With a menacing stalking motion she moved ever closer to the copse of trees.

Curious, both men followed behind the forceful dog. Falen moved quietly and closer to the pasture fence. Her voice lowered to a deep ominous sound as her muzzle twitched to and fro sampling the wind. As the odor got stronger, her mind registered where she'd noticed the stench before. It was the acrid smoke of the men from the roadside park. Men she hated, men who had tried to harm her master and Susan.

A cloud of dust skirted across the road. The red pickup tires squealed as Muscles jammed the gear into first spewing rocks and pebbles across the highway.

"That's somebody in a hurry." Walter picked up Falen's lead. "What do you think got Falen's back all up?"

"I'm not sure but I think it was the two guys I told you about, that hassled us at the Roadside Park. Falen charged and bit one of them before they could climb back into their truck."

He reached over and took the leash from Walt. "She did release when I told her to, otherwise we'd have a human leg for a trophy."

Falen trotted along beside Rick and Walt as they crossed the pasture back closer to the house. Her head was spinning, her thoughts a jumbled mess.

"Did I do what was right?" She stopped short to get a look at a crawling bug, then continued on a step or two in front of the men. *"I can tell smell of danger and I discern the odor of evil. Both of those humans are up to no good as far as I am concerned."* Looking up at Rick she stated, *"Don't worry Master, I know what to do the next time we see those two."* She gave a little Aussie chirp and danced along in front.

"She is so smart and advanced I don't think she will need any formal training, not after you told me about her 'virtually answering the phone'. I have some info sheets back in my office I will send you and if you work with her about 20 minutes a day I think you will be surprised in her advancement. I tell you Rick, that is a special dog you have, and with your continued improvement the two of you should get along just fine."

Falen smiled and Rick beamed, "Thanks so much, Walt. I really appreciate it and look forward to seeing you again. Maybe we can share a lunch when I get back to Bozeman?" Falen looked after the car exiting the driveway. Her eyes shone brightly in the afternoon sunshine. She knew this was a good day.

Twenty-Nine

Rick climbed the stairs of the front porch and plopped into the green chair that had become a replacement for his wheelchair. With a big smile Rick said to Falen, "Damned wheelchair." he said, "It's packed away for good."

Falen collapsed at his feet worn out from the stress of training and the heightened anxiety of her encounter with a threat. She didn't know where the smelly men had gone, she was just happy to be rid of them.

"Well, old girl, we had quite a workout didn't we?"

The red Aussie looked up at the sound of his voice and murfed a reply, *"Yes Master, even though I have four legs, all the running and trying to please, left me in need of a little nap."* At which she rested her red head on her two white paws and quickly she dove into dream land.

A gentle mountain breeze made its way down and across the verdant pasture caressing the two occupants on the Gonzales porch.

As Falen dozed in the cooling air, Rick kept running over in his mind what to make of the red truck tearing off like a bat out of hell. He wondered about those two men who agitated Falen so much she seemed prepared to attack?

"Well," he mused, "I can't let my imagination run away with me. This isn't a war zone, and I don't have to be on guard all the time." He glanced down at his legs, which gave him a reason to smile because of the freedom his new prosthetic gave him.

The breeze bathed his face; his eyes took in all of the beauty in front of him. The trees seemed to stand at attention while the birds flew an honor guard over the yard. He had come a long way from the angry young wounded warrior in constant despair over his affliction, and convinced that his life would never be the same. Now with the love of his life asleep at his feet, his mind wandered into a state of thankfulness. Pleased with his progress, in deep gratitude to his wonderful family, enthralled with the reunion of his relationship with Susan, and the prospects for a future as bright as the Montana sunshine, Rick's thoughts manifested themselves into a wide grin across his sunburned face.

As the sun slid over the peaks of the Absaroka Mountains, the sharp ringing of the phone snapped him out of his reverie. Falen immediately jumped up ready to assist in any way she was needed. Rick walked as briskly as possible, not quite sure of himself on the artificial leg.

Before he got out a hello, Susan started talking a mile a minute.

"Whoa there cowgirl, slip a rope around your ninety-mile-an-hour tongue and take a deep breath. Start again, this time in English." His grin slashed across his face, broad enough to light a normal-sized room. He loved every moment with Susan, even those precious moments when it was just the two of them on the phone.

When he didn't get a laugh in return he grew more serious and waited for her to begin speaking again.

"I just ran into Deputy Tom Hampton outside my dad's office, and what he had to say frightened me a bit."

Before Rick could interject, she continued.

"Tommy said the Sheriff's department was looking for a red Ford pickup that sounded a lot like the truck we encountered at the rest stop."

"Did he say why?"

Susan drew in a deep breath adding, "The two men who apparently own it are wanted for questioning for a robbery of some campers in the National Forest." Rick detected a catch in her voice. "The man they robbed was pretty badly beaten up. His wife had some minor cuts but the little boy and the couple's dog were so badly hurt the child is at Pioneer Medical Center and the pup is with Doc Kainer."

Susan choked back a sob and continued, "Sgt. Hampton checked at Dad's office to find out if we had insured a truck like it or had seen one fitting that description around these parts lately."

Rick's alarm button sounded and Falen intensified her focus on her master's face and demeanor, sensing Rick's heart rate rising. His mind flashed on the red truck across the road that stormed off in a hurry this afternoon. He didn't tell Susan about it because it might upset her even more.

Rick breathed more evenly trying to maintain his composure. He shuddered at the fact that they could have been in mortal danger that rainy day back in Bozeman.

Susan paused, sobbed again, and before she resumed talking, Rick interrupted. "Susan, don't worry. I'll call Tommy at the Sheriff's office and add any information I can to what you told him. These guys have to be caught before someone else is hurt." He glanced at his new Toyota Sequoia. He was learning to trust his artificial leg when driving, but he recognized the different pressure on the gas pedal and brake. This was no time to worry about that; he wanted to rush to Susan's side as fast as he could.

"Are you still at your Dad's agency?"

"Yes."

"Stay there. I'll be up in a minute or so." He opened the door of the vehicle, told Falen to "mount up", and drove as quickly as possible toward Big Timber.

Thirty

Susan stared at her cell phone for what seemed like an eternity. She was terrified for the first time in her adult life. The past months had brought her the happiness she'd longed for all of her life. Her close relationship with her father anchored her life, and the reunion with Rick made her personal dreams seem so real. Now this, a direct threat to the harmony of her inner circle, caused by two angry men who had entered her consciousness only a short three weeks ago.

The Sequoia screeched to a stop in the no parking space just outside the front door to Burton's Insurance Agency. Rick climbed down, hurrying to get to Susan.

"Hey Girl", he said as the door to the office closed behind him. "Suz, don't worry, we are going to figure this all out, and believe me, Tommy and the Sheriff's office will find these hoodlums before anyone else is hurt."

Falen jumped out of the window of the SUV and nosed her way into the office. Rick, so used to having her with him absently reached down and rubbed her head more out of habit than reassurance. Susan pet Falen's white neck letting the touch of her fingers ply through the thick fur. To be able to connect with the Aussie had become a source of comfort to both of them. Falen's eyes darted between her people, looking for any trace of tension or fear in Rick or Susan's face.

The Aussie's alert eyes saw Cecil Burton enter the room. It was like Falen cleared her throat to announce the presence of someone else in the room.

"Hey, you two", Cecil reached out to shake hands with Rick, while he placed his other hand on his daughter's shoulder. The elder Burton had always liked Rick, had watched him excel in sports, and was genuinely grieved at the news of Rick's battlefield injury. His marriage to LaNelle had grown indifferent over the years. He poured himself into his work, and when his only child decided to forego Chicago and return to help him with the business, his spirits had never been higher. Now trouble surrounded her. Cecil, ever the protector, concentrated all of his attention on her fears. 'Burtons' protect Burtons', was his motto, and Susan had always counted on him. Now she stood in a room with both of the strong men in her life. Their mere presence calmed her.

Nearly every family in Sweetgrass County shared this unrest. This friendly community welcomed strangers. A smile was the first thing, besides the natural beauty of the landscape most visitors remarked upon.

Other than the trouble Javier Coronado experienced when thugs tried to burn down his ranch, Sweetgrass remained a peaceful and productive place to live. In any area attractive to tourists, it's hard trying to keep up with all of the strange faces. Now this danger surrounding the two men suspected of beating and robbing a family camping in the wilderness sharpened each person's awareness. The Sheriff's department was on high alert, especially with all of the 4th of July activities planned.

Out on the sidewalk again Rick tried to sooth Susan's shattered nerves. "How about you and me, and Falen makes three," Rick paused to laugh at his own joke, "head over to Livingston and munch some lunch at the Sport?"

"I don't know. I look a mess, and I'm not sure I can keep anything down if I eat."

She glanced up the street looking for anything or anybody that didn't fit.

Rick could feel the tension in her arms. Falen could, too, so she reached up and gave her hand a firm, juicy lick, as if to say, "There, now, it's going to be alright."

Rick's tender gaze broke through her fear and Susan started breathing a bit more slowly. Falen pushed against her leg urging her on. Susan gave in. "Falen girl, if you think this will do us some good, let's mount up and ride."

Rick held the door for his two girls, as the red head bounded into the back seat, and the dark-haired beauty got in the front seat. No one talked on the ride into town, except for the occasional whine or bark, if Falen noticed anything she wasn't sure of. A peaceful day can have a darkened underbelly when the presence of danger is in the air.

Thirty-One

"I can't wait for the Ringling Five to sing "We Share Montana". Rick shut his truck door and stepped up on the sidewalk still talking about the Ringling Five. "I carried one of their CD's with me all over Afghanistan. Sure helped drive the 'willies' away at night." He laughed.

"I'm looking forward to seeing them in person", Susan answered as she reached the front door of the Sport Café, and slipped through the door Rick held open for her. She pulled off her sunglasses to let her eyes get accustomed to the interior. With the exception of the unrest caused by the two militia men, Susan Burton never felt better in her life. Her eyes glowed as she took in the image of her Marine. Rick grew more confident with his artificial leg as the weeks zoomed by. If you didn't know, you would never take him for a person with a prosthetic limb.

"Well, look at this handsome couple." Nick Esp, the owner of the famous eatery, stood just to the left of the main bar, right under the antlers hanging on the wall, and walked over to greet them.

"How're you doing, Rick? You seem ready to take on the world since you got home."

It's got to be all those Sport burgers I've woofed down lately." Rick patted his stomach and Susan blushed.

"How's your Dad, Susan?"

"Mean as ever, and constantly on me to work harder at the Agency instead of parading around with the Marine Corps."

Nick showed them to a table and left to get their drinks.

"We're becoming quite the couple around town." Rick smiled and added, "I love parading around with you, too." Susan fiddled with the saltshaker. Nick returned with two glasses of iced tea, and left them with menus, as if they needed them. Rather shyly Susan said, "Look, I don't mind being the third woman in your life, right after Isabelle and Falen." She sipped her tea and continued, "That is if you will have me, Mr. Marine? After all I've chased you since seventh grade." She beamed."

"I believe we'll be the cutest couple at the Rodeo." Rick smiled.

In only two weeks the biggest party in Montana, the Livingston 4th of July parade and rodeo, would turn the whole countryside into a giant hometown jamboree. In fact, one day wasn't enough for these partying Montanans. It took a full three days to celebrate their freedom and love for this land.

"Hey, you two, how you doing?" Sheriff's Deputy Tommy Hampton took off his hat and eased over to the table.

"Tommy, grab a chair and join us", Rick pulled the third chair from the table, and Tommy slid in. "What brings you to Livingston, and out of your county?"

"Not much. Just a large case of the 'can't waits' for the 4th's merrymaking." The waiter asked if he might get anything for the lawman. Tommy motioned to Rick and Susan's iced teas, and said, "I'll have what these two hard drinkers are having."

Rick grew more serious and changed the subject. "What's up with those two guys in the red truck? Do you think they were the culprits who harassed the family camping?"

"We're pretty sure it was them, but with the size of the counties here, and the vastness of the National Forest, they might be holed up anywhere in these mountains."

The deputy shifted in his seat. "We're doing everything we can, and so are the Feds.

We've got a tri-county task force using our facilities; Park and Gallatin counties have officers looking at every spot a human might hide in these woods. The state even provided helicopter flybys, trying to find them. We'll get them, I'm sure. I just hope it's before they hurt someone else or destroy someone's property.

Susan shuddered at the thought of those two and how close she and Rick had come to a confrontation on that rainy day. Her hand dropped to pet Falen before she realized that the Aussie had been left in the truck.

Her mind eased at the thought of the loyalty of the dog, and how much Falen meant to Rick, and now her.

Deputy Hampton finished his tea, excused himself, and headed back down to Sweetgrass. Rich had a nervous flutter in the pit of his stomach. It was the same sensation he had over and over in battle. He wasn't sure what was going to happen, but he knew he was up to any danger that was presented. After the encounter at the tourist stop, he believed Susan and he were in the gun sights of the criminals.

Nothing is so dark as the forest when the sun descends over the mountains. The small fire gave a little light as Muscles and Weiner sipped another cup of bourbon. After a trip out of county to the liquor store near the interstate, both were pretty well stocked up on 'hooch', as they referred to it.

"This shindig these folks is planning is really something. Cowboys come to the rodeo from all over the country and most of the people take a full three days off and party, brother, party."

A snap of a twig drew their attention; both quieted and stared into the darkness. Nothing moved, no sounds were heard. Finally, Muscles broke the silence. "You think with so many people at the parade and rodeo, we could make us a little money helping ourselves to some of their goodies while they're away."

Weiner grunted, "Help myself to more than trinkets, if I find one of their women at home alone." Weiner broke himself up with that remark. He laughed so hard spittle ran down the sides of his mouth.

Several minutes passed before Muscles heard another sound like scraping on a rock. The sound jolted them both upright. Whispering, he said, "Do you think somebody's out there?"

More silence as the pair strained their eyes staring into the darkness. A nagging doubt troubled both men. They may not be alone. Neither of them wanted to venture out into the darkened forest. The booze hadn't given them enough courage.

Thirty-Two

The glare in her yellow eyes was enough to frighten the youngsters back into submission. She didn't have to make a sound. Her gaze was severe enough. At over a hundred and thirty pounds Sheena didn't ever disturb any of the forest when she moved from place to place. Especially when hunting, she moved with silence and grace. Now her two cubs apparently hadn't learned the same lesson.

Her life mate, the majestic Timber Wolf, Steele, never took his eyes off of the two men huddled around the campfire. Sheena's rebuking gaze seemed sufficient to still the clatter from the two pups. The breaking of the twig and the scratch by one of the pups trying to climb a rock to get a better view, alerted the two humans, but seemed quickly forgotten. In Sheena's mind it could not be allowed again. Not if these two pups, nearly a year old, grew into the maturity wolves need to survive in the Absaroka Mountains.

Sheena tested the air for scent of the two outsiders.

Her lips curled in disgust as her nose filled with stale cigarette stench and sour booze. Deep in her sub-conscious, a vile memory of her tormentor, Ron Spencer, turned her stomach. A small guttural growl slipped through her clenched teeth. Steele noticed, but kept his eyes focused on the humans, looking for any furtive movement. Neither pup made any more moves or sounds. They loved their mother, but were afraid of her wrath.

The bitter memory of her treatment under Spencer never left her. She learned that some humans appeared safe, and protective of animals, like the people her adopted son, Bandit, lived with. She also knew of a trait in humans that could cause havoc on the lives of 'dumb animals', to use a 'people' expression.

A gust of wind fanned the embers into flames, lighting the area around the campfire, as if an electric light had been turned on. Muscles glanced up over the rim of his cup of bourbon into the dull eyes of his cohort in crime. Both men were filthy from weeks in the mountains trying to elude the manhunt. Their courage and bravado was artificially fueled by massive doses of alcohol. The effect of all the drinking, and a minimal intake of food heightened the inbred paranoia consuming both men. Everyone seemed out to get them. The rich and powerful teamed with the politically controlling to hold both men, and their families, down, and keep them poor. In their minds there were millions of folks just like them. At every corner of their lives someone or something seemed to be after them. This time would be different. Weiner vowed to make a stand for freedom against all of the natives in Sweetgrass County. Muscles agreed, and they planned to wreak havoc on the so-called good citizens, and then move on the North Dakota for a planned meeting of like-minded militia men and white supremacists. Both men looked forward to the overthrow of the United States Government.

Weiner refilled his cup with whisky. The booze dulled his judgment, causing him to speak too loudly. He started to rise up from the ground and proclaim his intent to the world. "I fight for right and might, and I'll slay any sucker that gets in my way."

'He stumbled a bit and quickly righted himself. "We'll show these corn pones what a 4th of July celebration should be as we march through this valley takin' ever-thing we want, and killing those who dare to stop us.

For two warriors out on a mission, they were poorly equipped. From an outdoor store over the state line in Colorado, they had burglarized, their stash was two pistols, a .22 caliber rifle, a tranquilizer gun, and several boxes of ammunition for all three weapons. Not quite enough to hold off the team of Sweetgrass County deputies or the Federal Rangers, who were in hot pursuit.

Less than fifty feet from the campground stood Sheena and her family. On guard against anything or anyone bent on destroying their home, both mature wolves appeared content to wait and see what these strangers were up to.

Without turning, Sheena whispered to Steele, *"Let's take the boys back to the den and when they are safe, I'll come back and guard through the night. In case these humans plan to harm us, I will howl a warning, and you can quickly join me."*

Steele took the lead with Sheena and the pups in silent formation. Trailing behind, one of the pups whispered to his brother, *"I hope the Spirit of the Night and Day will protect our Mom tonight.*

Thirty-Three

The night chill wasn't the only thing sending shivers through the survivalists. The dense forest appeared much more foreboding than either imagined, when they planned this venture back in Oklahoma. The supermarket magazine racks were filled with articles painting an idyllic picture of living free in the wilderness without owing any man or government for the privilege.

After spending two weeks hiding out in the Absaroka Mountains, this idea of living on their own had become a bitter pill. Booze could offer only so much courage. Now they realized that the forest was populated with numerous life-threatening perils. Both men knew they were stuck in this gamble for fear of the other militia members, who might frown on their cowardice.

Muscles heaved a sigh, spit into the fire, and tried to reassure his companion of the rightness of their mission.

"Listen to me, Weiner. I got this gut feeling that the brothers are depending on us to make this whole plan work." Weiner picked up a twig and poked the coals of the campfire. "Back home we got sick and tired of how the so-called 'nice folks' treated us, all because we're dirt poor, and born into families living on the edgy side of life."

"Yeah, I guess you're right," he said, as he looked at the man he'd known since childhood.

Born to an unwed mother, addicted to every illegal substance, Winston Charles Woodmaker grew up extremely malnourished. The lack of proper nutrition stifled his growth, leaving him a skinny sunken-faced kid. His appearance alone kept him from making friends. Plus having no spending money, force him to live a friendless life. At about 12 years old a new boy moved into his town. He was just as down and out as Winston seemed to be. Also, he had been further burdened at having to live down the name that had been bestowed on him at birth. Woodrow Wilson Weiner became the butt of other kids' humor. 'Wittle Weird Weiner' became the albatross hanging around his neck. Winston Charles suffered from the same kind of mocking for his slight frame by calling him 'Muscles'. The boys instantly became partners in misery. Against the harangue from the 'better' group of kids, the two misfits bonded, and swore to watch each other's back for life.

Always traveling together kept most of the physical danger away, but the taunting, and name-calling continued throughout their schooling, until they both dropped out in the 11th grade. Both tried to enlist in the Army, as a way of getting their lives in order, but physical ailments, and deformities because of the malnutrition barred both of them from a military career.

The hatred boiled up against any form of authority and fed a life of petty crime and multiple arrests. Finally, after many odd jobs, and run-ins with the law, they finally met some like-minded and kindred spirits in a group of outcasts called the East Woods Patriots. Most of the members had prison records. A few had milked the system for all it was worth, and the rest were a handful of wanna-be's, like Woodmaker and Weiner.

After months of conversations about how the two misfits might be the sparkplugs in building a new 'white only' community in the badlands of the Dakotas', Weiner and Muscles set off for Montana to try to steal enough money and goods to stake the new compound. Neither ever thought their compatriots were only making sport of them, so they undertook this so-called mission to heart with pride and passion. It is safe to say that most of the militia members back in Oklahoma had already erased these two from their minds.

This night the pretend patriots' only audience were the yellow eyes of Sheena. She stood sentry about 20 yards outside the light of the fire, silent and watchful.

Thirty-Four

Fear didn't enter the mind of Falen as she snoozed in the sunshine that filled her favorite spot on the Gonzales' front porch. What bothered her this morning was a pesky fly using her nose as landing strip.

The red-headed girl looked on as her master, Rick, drove out of the driveway. She assumed he was on his way to pick up Susan. With nothing to do but watch the calves graze in the front pasture, the Aussie decided to close her amber eyes and turn her brain over to the Spirit of the Day and Night. Dreams flooded her mind and heart with thoughts of love for Rick and the whole family. Falen often dreamed of laying her red head down in Susan's lap in a meadow filled with wild flowers. Susan wore Fendi cologne with a flower base so natural, that Falen would associate any floral scent with her dear friend.

Falen's only venture into the forest was the time she had helped herd the livestock, and had had her encounter with the renegade wolf. Most of the day she had kept to the pastureland as the cattle moved to the higher grazing grounds.

True, she remembered listening wide-eyed as her brother, Bandit, told of his time with the wolf dog, Sheena, in the wild. Bandit had a special gleam in his eyes, letting the rest of the dogs know that he had seen things they could only dream about. Bandit's courage and fearlessness covered his family like a blanket, stimulating all of those around him with a sense of calm and safety; especially after he and the Pyrenees saved the ranch from the criminals bent on burning it down. Fallen lived in her brother's shadow, and worshipped the ground he walked on. Even here at the Gonzales ranch, several miles from the Townsend Sheep and Cattle Company, she imagined her big brother somehow looked after her, and prayed with her for the peace and protection of the Spirit of the Day and Night.

Miles away in the Absaroka Mountains Sheena kept up her guard over the two intruders. The wolf's keen senses warned her of the danger of these two humans. The reek of tobacco and body odor sent chills through her, causing a horrible memory of her days of captivity at Ron Spencer's so-called kennel. One of the few things that frightened Sheena was fire. So she studied the campers and their casual way of tending the constant wood flames. At that time of year, a spark misplaced could cause the entire area to burst into a forest fire. If a fire started Sheena wanted to be able to run away with her pups and her love, the mighty Steele.

It's hard to be safe with a booze-addled brain. Weiner and Muscles were slow to wake. The brilliance of the sun caused their heads to hurt even more than the poison in their bodies from another night of drinking. Muscles stumbled over to the coffee pot resting on a rock near the embers of last night's blaze. A small rock rolled beneath his shoe causing him to fall head first into the dying embers. His shirt started to ignite. "Shit, Weiner, help me put out this fire on my shirt before I go up in flames."

His companion threw the remains of a glass of liquor on him not thinking the alcohol would cause the flame to blaze even more. Muscles danced around screaming and beating the spot on his chest, yelling "Damn it, Weiner, I'm about to burn up." The embers on his shirt never grew into a flame, and after several hard swipes at the spot, the threat vanished.

Exhausted from all the jumping and dancing, Muscle collapsed near his bedroll and, wiping the sweat from his face said, "I've just about had it with this wild woodsman stuff." He glanced again at the dark spot on his chest, "If'n we don't git our shit together and git out of here, we might as well give up."

"We can't, Muscles. We'd have hell to pay from those others in the group. We'd be failures and no goods, just like we been for most of our lives. This here is a way to make something of ourselves. We gotta stick this thing through."

Muscle's face furrowed into a frown as he reached for a cigarette, which he lit before he answered. Inhaling deeply and letting the smoke sift out through his nose he sighed, "I guess you're right, but I will tell you this. When we finally get to North Dakota I ain't about to go into any more Goddamned, God-forsaken woods, no siree."

Weiner's laughter could be heard through- out the still forest. "Woods, what in Hell's Bells do you think North Dakota is? Shit man, it ain't hardly got no woods. You're going to live in grassland prairie, where the nearest tree is over a mile away. Man, about the highest thing you're gonna see is a sidewalk, if'n they got any of those." Weiner barely got out the words due to his laughing fit.

Sheena stared at the duo, unable to figure out whether this was some kind of a dance or they were getting ready to attack. Her piercing eyes held nothing but contempt for this pair. She thanked the Spirit of the Day and Night she didn't have to live among their kind anymore.

Thirty-Five

"Hey kiddo, want to go out tonight and do a little dancin'?

Susan didn't control her enthusiasm. She threw her arms around Rick's neck and spouted out a series of "YES, YES, YES!"

"Nothing fancy you know, I'm not sure whether or not a spin or a twirl wouldn't get me a little off kilter." Rick gazed into her eyes and added, "But if this Montana Cowgirl is willing, I'll try to keep up on Uncle Sam's plastic leg."

Falen joined in the ecstasy and did her version of dancin' around the couple.

"I guess you're not going to take me, huh? I'm going to have to stay home again, but let me tell you, if it's going to be fun, I need to be there."

The whole conversation from Falen sounded to Rick and Susan like a series of high-pitched yaps, but they understood. Understanding Falen was a matter of paying attention.

The threesome's excitement was being shared in every ranch and home from Bozeman to Big Timber and beyond. This year the 4th landed on a Thursday, which insured the party would start on the 2nd and 3rd with the conclusion on the national holiday. While the parade and Rodeo were the main attraction, the entire countryside geared up for the music, shows and the fabulous food filling the streets. 'Out of Towners' flooded the area, all looking for the authentic American experience that's been going on since the 1920's. Sergio and Isabelle had been invited to ride in the float sponsored by the American Legion of Big Timber. Sergio had been an active member ever since he returned from his Army Duty in Korea. Devoted to the work and mission of the Legion, he sported a new Legionnaires cap, and not to be outdone, Isabelle spared no expense on her festival dress from one of the best stores in Bozeman. Rick and Susan planned to join her father in front of the Murray Hotel.

The Livingston Roundup Rodeo and Parade announced the official start of summer in this beautiful valley and neighboring mountains. Just like the burst of flowers and trees the population was ready to rid themselves of the winter blues and welcome another warm and lazy summertime.

Muscles had picked up a morning copy of the Livingston Enterprise when he snuck into Big Timber that morning trying to procure some food. All of the celebration plans and parade routes were laid out with advertising about the best places to eat, stay and party.

"Seems to me like all of these yahoos are gonna be partying and whooping it up for about three days, and partner of mine, you know what that means, don't you?"

Weiner faked a blank stare on his face and replied, "No Mister Information, why don't you just enlighten me."

Muscles didn't get the joke and proceeded. "Well, I will tell ya, all of this ruckus means very few of these so called "Big Time Cowboys" will be at home. They'll probably leave their houses and barn's open to the likes of me and you. We can clean up, and be headed to North Dakota faster than a rabbit in heat."

"I get the picture. We'll hit, load up and run with enough loot to please our brother patriots. Then we can live in peace among white people just like us."

Muscles turned the page of the paper and said, "Hey, look at this. It seems some of those redskins over North Dakota way are protesting about us setting up a white-only village."

"Hell man, we whupped them Indians once, we can do it again." He spit in the direction of the dying fire, "This is our land, born free, white and independent. We ain't gonna let a few ne'er-do well Indians keep us from our goal."

This news called for another round of whiskey, which set off an afternoon of drinking that lead to another drunken night.

Steele took over so Sheena could feed the pups. He growled under his breath. It took every bit of restraint for the Timber Wolf not to attack, so bitter was his hatred of these two humans.

Thirty-Six

A gentle breeze fluttered the American flag posted on the mailbox of the Gonzales Ranch. Up and down the highways of this area of Montana, flags and other patriotic emblems and posters represented the enthusiasm building up in the residents.

Rick drove into Big Timber to pick up some supplies for the ranch and some grocery items for his mom. He wore his marine fatigues and was surprised by the many people who both saluted and said, "Nice job, Marine" or "Thanks for your service."

Little did the passersby realize the sacrifice Rick had made. By now he was so adept at walking with his artificial limb, the average person would never guess he didn't have two strong legs. Falen marched at Rick's side and smiled at all of the people acknowledging Rick.

Bunting and decorations lined all of the streets in Big Timber as well as posters announcing the Rodeo and Roundup scheduled three days away. Some of the stores and shops along the streets in Big Timber played recorded patriotic music.

"Hey, Corporal, you're looking mighty fit and fine this morning. Want to grab a cup of coffee?" Deputy Tommy Hampton, just going on patrol, had a few minutes to chat with Rick. Both men loved the fun of the 4th of July celebration, but also realized it was a perfect opportunity for anyone planning mischief. They weren't too far from Johnny's Java, plus Rick could leave Falen in the SUV, and keep an eye on her while they visited.

The two men had been friends since high school. When Rick joined the Marines, Tommy was already a Deputy Sheriff and decided to serve his country in the Montana National Guard. Both respected each other's service.

After about ten minutes of chit chat, Tommy brought up an unpleasant subject.

"With more and more folks coming in from out of state, it's beginning to be a hardship on us to keep the peace."

Rick sipped from his mug of coffee, "I can only imagine. We've become so complacent because of our many years of peaceful times. You can't judge strangers by how they look. Heck, man, most people dress so sloppy now-a-days they might pass for someone just out of the slammer." Both smiled as a teenager passed their table with his pants so low his underwear was sticking up about two inches.

In a serious vein Rick inquired, "What about those two who hassled Susan and I at the road side park?"

"We now have a pretty good idea they're the guilty parties in the robbery and beating of the family in the National Park. We've had a slew of reports of petty theft of ranches and business and have an APB (All points Bulletin) out for the red truck they've been seen driving. In fact, we got a stolen truck request from the state police in Oklahoma about it about three weeks ago."

Tommy stopped talking to acknowledge a man passing their table. He continued lowering his voice a little, "You're as familiar with this country as anyone. If a person wants to get lost in the mountains it's pretty darn easy. We've put out posters all around the tourist stops and camping areas, hoping someone will see them and tip us off."

"I know Tommy, and with all of the visitors here for the 4th, it's going to make the hunt even harder. I told you about the red truck parked across from my Dad's place. We were out working Falen when she started acting funny. She usually is in such a happy mood, but she noticed the strange truck before we did, got her back up and was ready to tear into anybody that tried to bother us."

Rick, I think you are becoming more attached to that dog than to most people, Susan excepted." Both laughed. Rick turned a little red.

"Ninety nine bottles of beer on the wall, ninety nine bottles of beer." The Explorer rocked with the boisterous voices of the Simons family.

This was the fourth day of their car trip, bound for Livingston, Montana, so the Senior Simons could treat the growing family to an authentic American commemoration. Roger Simons' father moved to California from Winnett, Montana before Roger Jr. was born. The old man regaled the children with tales of the Wild West, the mighty plains of Montana, and the most beautiful mountains in the world. Twice Roger accompanied his family back to the big sky country, and grew up believing if there was a Heaven, it had to be in Montana. With Marietta and the brood of California surfers on board, Roger supposed the family's Americana trip would leave a lasting imprint on their lives. As they left Interstate 15 for a side trip through the mighty Yellowstone National Park, the blasé teenagers turned into real explorers and with their cell phones were photographing everything in sight. Roger beamed, and couldn't believe his good fortune. His work kept him away from home a lot of the time, and the trip's togetherness cemented his family's relationship.

The Simons' had been traveling steady for about four hours since entering Yellowstone, and now the familiar cries of "Daddy can't we stop. I've got to go to the bathroom" wedded with "I'm hungry, and Stop it, you're pushing on me." Without turning her head Marietta said, "Be Quiet!" "Your father will stop at Paradise Bed and Breakfast, just up ahead. We are going to see if they have any accommodations for us"

That seemed to settle it, and they returned to another chorus of "Ninety nine bottles of beer."

No one in the Explorer noticed the rickety red truck following for the last thirty minutes.

Thirty-Seven

"Paradise is one of the wonderful places to stay in this part of the country. Shoot, if I have time, I might get in a little fly-fishing."

Marietta was bending back over the front seat trying to separate two of the kids engaged in a pushing fight.

"Good for you, but the kids and I want to spend some time getting souvenirs in Livingston."

In a chorus came multiple sentences from the back seat. "Mom promised us." "Yeah, I want some real Indian moccasins." All blended with "When are we going to stop?"

Roger had to shout over the noise, "This resort is only 32 minutes from Livingston, so I am sure we all can get to do our favorite things."

The scenery was so awe-inspiring the occupants of the Simon van didn't pay any attention to the red pickup pulling up closer behind them.

By the time Roger turned off into the resort, the pair in the truck passed them as if they were on a routine trip to Livingston.

All of the Simons' noses were plastered against the windows as they maneuvered the drive to the main Lodge House. Multitudes of flowers graced the landscape. The rustic buildings held a warm welcome to all who entered.

"This place is named correctly. If this isn't paradise, I don't know where it would be?" As the Explorer eased to a stop, the family poured out of the doors eager to escape the confinement of auto travel.

"I've 'really-really' got to go to the bathroom," the oldest girl shouted as she ran up the walkway to the lodge.

Carol Reed was waiting at the open door ready to greet the travelers like she'd done so many times before. Marietta sighed. This may well be the quiet rest she's been needing for a long time. "Ah, Peace", she exclaimed to herself.

Out on the main highway the red truck that had followed them for over an hour had pulled over to the shoulder.

"Weiner, you got everything we need?" Muscles was pilfering around in the bed of the truck. "Yep, got the license plate we stole and the wrenches to add it to that new Ford. You got our fire power?"

"Yessiree! Locked and loaded as we American warriors like to say."

They climbed back into the truck, turned around and drove back toward the entrance of the resort.

"After settling in their cabin, Roger and Marietta decided on a quick trip into Livingston would be just the ticket to wash away their travel sores. Two of the older kids opted to stay in the cabin to explore the grounds. The youngest decided to go with their parents in hope of getting to buy something.

The Ford Explorer headed back toward highway 89 for a quick ride into Livingston. They turned onto the highway and didn't get too far before both Roger and Marietta noticed a red truck disabled on the side of the road. One man with his back toward the oncoming cars held up a cardboard sign with the words 'HELP US' in large red letters. Rodger slid to a stop and parked just behind the stranded truck.

"Stay here. Let me try to help this guy." He exited the driver's door and walked toward the man with the sign.

"Hey there, do you need help?" Roger laughed to himself about how dumb that must sound to someone who has been holding up a sign saying, "Help".

"Yes sir, much obliged. My friend in the cab is awful sick and I can't get this thing started to drive him in to a hospital."

Without facing Roger the scruffy man started walking toward the passenger's door to the truck. Roger followed. Standing by the door, he said, "If'n you help me get him up, maybe a breath of fresh air would do him good."

Through the truck window Roger saw another man sprawled out on the bench seat. Muscles stepped aside so Roger could reach in to help sit the man up. The minute his hand reached Weiner's shoulder, Roger found himself starring into the barrel of a nine-millimeter pistol.

"You make one sound or move at all, and you will be breathing through a whole different hole in your head." Muscles grabbed Roger's arms in a bear hug while

Weiner held the gun. The trio slowly eased away from the truck, making sure they stayed out of eyesight from the passengers in the green SUV.

"No noise, no yelling out or your family will get to watch their Daddy getting shot dead on the side of the road."

Terrified, Roger held his breath. He knew it would be futile to try to disarm these bandits. Thinking he could stall for time in order to figure out how to save his family, he tried to remain calm and quiet.

Marietta had given into her daughter, Lisa, who had chosen to come with them, and turned on the CD player with some of their favorite raucous kids songs. She didn't hear any of the conversation from outside near the truck, and assumed Roger would return, and they would be on their way. She looked up through the windshield as Roger was being marched toward the car with two very desperate looking men holding a gun on him.

She said in a very quiet voice, "Lisa, be still and turn off the player. Daddy's in trouble."

Thirty-Eight

Roger held Lisa tight as the family watched their car pull out and head north. Stranded and frightened, the Simons family decided to walk the miles back to Paradise Gateway Resort.

"I think it's about a two hour walk", he patted Lisa's head as she cried.

"Roger, don't worry, we'll make it. I am so proud of you, and the way you handled those criminals. You saved our lives." Marietta was on the verge of tears herself.

"This is one sweet ride, thanks to old man Ford". With all of the forces of the combined Park County, Sweetgrass and Gallatin Sheriff's offices on high alert, it seemed only a matter of time before the pair would be apprehended. In the meantime however, the militia members roamed the Big Sky country creating fear in the hearts of residents and visitors, especially in the wake of the biggest annual celebration in Southwestern Montana.

The patrol car from the Park County Sheriff's office screeched to a halt in front of the resort's main building. A 'be on the lookout for' had been broadcast to all law enforcement officers in the area. After Deputy Manual took the report from the distraught Simon family he immediately drove back on US 89 in search of the bandits. Tommy Hampton in his Sweetgrass Sheriff's patrol car responded to the bulletin and agreed to meet Manual right outside of Livingston.

"Hey Lew, how is that family holding up?" Manuel exited his patrol car and with an out stretched hand replied, "Tommy, as good as can be expected. They went through a pretty rough time with those two, but at least I got a good description of our subjects. The little girl with them snapped a picture of them before it dawned on her how serious this incident was. Tommy shook hands with his old friend.

"Your office must be on high alert with all of the 4th celebrations in a couple of days, and the thousands of tourists showing up."

Manuel laughed, "A lot of those tourists just want to get a glimpse of Peter Fonda if they can." He leaned against the car and continued, "On a serious note however, our obligation to keep all of the visitors and our own people safe is the number one priority. Who knows what these crazy bastards might do."

The conversation was interrupted by the police radio.

"Attention all units, Suspects' car has been spotted leaving US 89 and headed up into the National Forest."

"Hell's Bells, Weiner, we lucked out this time. This is a four-wheel drive chariot which is a lot better than that old truck we had."

"Yeah, and we ain't got no stickers all over this one making us so easy to track."

Muscles turned the green Explorer onto a little-used fire road that would take them up to their campsite. Both were sure their location was hidden enough in the woods that they couldn't be spotted by copters flying over. The road, cluttered with large rocks and fallen timber, didn't deter the vehicle's progress.

"If'n we're ever gonna run for it, this baby is sure going to come in handy."

From a vantage point about a couple of hundred feet up the mountain from the make- shift campsite, Sheena and Steele saw the progress of the car. Both wolves were looking for the return of the red truck, and the nasty pair they had come to hate. But duly noted by both, the green car had no business in this part of the forest.

Miles away at the Gonzales Ranch Falen dozed on the front porch in her favorite spot where the sun warmed her, and she could enjoy the light breeze. The excitement her family enjoyed about the upcoming Livingston Rodeo and Parade seeped into this Aussie, although she didn't really know why. Her main joy was the lack of stress she noted in Rick. The new leg, the love of Susan, and the warmth of the Gonzales family all combined to make her master calm and happy. When Rick was happy, Falen was happy. Life in southwestern Montana couldn't have been better.

Falen Five

I sometimes forget to thank the Spirit of the Day and Night for my life. Rick provides all my needs, food, water, shelter and a generous amount of love, so I never want for anything. It's amazing how having everything you need in life draws you away from the habit of talking to the source of our lives, The Spirit of the Day and Night.

Bandit, my brother and my hero, told us of the almost daily occurrences when the Spirit of the Day and Night protected his adopted mother, Sheena, from the dangers of the deep forest. The weather is a constant source of danger when you live in the wild. Other animals bent on killing for their food prowled the pair. The fight for territory and shelter remained constant. Existence proved to be a daily chore.

When winter is too cold here on our ranch I snuggle up next to Rick in his warm bed and sleep the night away in peace. I've never had a hunger pain in my life, and if I get cut or scratched, off we go to Dr. Kainer's.

Oh, I still remember to include the Spirit of the Day and Night in my thoughts, but I've never felt the closeness that Bandit describes. The Spirit of the Day and Night is one with my brother. You can almost sense the intimacy when we are together.

This morning these thoughts invaded my mind in the middle of my dream about how good things were going. I didn't think there could ever be an Aussie Dog as blessed as me. I must admit, I longed for the connection with the Spirit that Bandit enjoyed, but I was sure I didn't want to go through all of the harrowing experiences he did. Nope, I am a happy pup, content to enjoy all of the blessings coming to the

Aussie who was beloved by Rick Gonzales. The problem with being content is contentment seems to blind your view of the future.

Thirty-Nine

"Hal, you sure you don't want to go into town with us for all of the hoop-de-do?"

Sergio, dressed in his best western clothes stood outside the back of the house conversing with his trusted friend and assistant ranch boss.

Hal laughed, "No siree, when you've been to as many rodeo's as me and been kicked, bucked, trampled and rode over, the last place I find amusing is a pen with a lot of cowboys trying to make travel money. No sir, I am happy as that pup laying in the sun to stay here and look after things. This ranch is my world and I am too damned old to want to live it up again."

A sly grin creased Hal's weathered face. "Tell you the truth," he chuckled, "I lived it up enough for about eight cowboys. Rest and relaxation is my main goal now."

Before the elder Gonzales answered, Hal interjected, "If'n you had a mind to, you all might bring me some Bar-b-cue. I bet I can eat about five sandwiches."

Rick honked the SUV's horn to hurry up his father. Everyone else had dressed up, loaded up and was raring to go. Sergio always left his beloved ranch last. Rick blew the horn again as his father rounded the corner with a slew of "Hold you horses, Hold your horses, I'm coming. I had some important things to talk over with Hal."

The elder statesman of the Gonzales family grabbed the handle of the front door and swung up into the cab next to his son.

"What did you tell Hal, how to keep an eye out for lost cattle, or stray chickens?" Isabelle joined in the laugh. Sergio said, "For your information, mister smarty pants, I needed to find out how many pulled pork bar-b-cue sandwiches he wanted."

"That is important! I'll forgive you for making us late."

"Late? We've got three whole days ahead of us! How in thunder can we be late?"

Falen raised her head to stare at the family. She was used to the friendly squabbling. Satisfied all was well, she let her red head flop back on the porch.

Susan was standing out front when Rick pulled up. The sun filtering through the trees made a halo around her. Rick's eyes watered with pride. He so loved this young woman.

"Hey there, folks, ready to do some patriotic rodeoing?" Isabelle scooted over as Sergio piled into the back so Susan could ride up front with Rick.

The time was late in the day for most ranchers. It was still early in the morning for the city folk just getting up and getting ready for the day.

"What say we head over for some breakfast before the café gets too crowded?" Sergio, always ready to eat, seconded the motion. This was the beginning of a perfect day as far as all were concerned. Rick reached over for Susan's hand. A gentle squeeze and he put the car in gear. Already the streets were beginning to fill up with patrons. If Big Timber was this active they knew Livingston must be 'jumpin'.

Rick rolled down the car's window and yelled at Deputy Tommy Hampton, "Join us for breakfast." He added, "I'll buy." The deputy waved back, "You know I can't turn free food down. See ya there."

The morning made a different promise to Weiner and Muscles. Their hung over and tired bodies rolled out of the sleeping bags in their lean-to shelter. The embers of last night's fire were dead. Both didn't talk much but set about rebuilding the fire and making some coffee to wash away the cobwebs. As crisp and clear as the Montana sky appeared, crystal blue with a temperature of about forty-one degrees, the bright glare intensified their headaches. Muscles believed the 'hair of the dog' might straighten them out. Before the coffee boiled, they consumed two full cups of whiskey. Quickly the booze dulled their minds again, so they felt normal.

"Gist like you said, most of these goobers have up and left for the festivities, leaving houses and homes ripe for our picking."

Weiner got a gleam of delight in his bloodshot eyes. "Man, if'n we make us a haul, load down that Ford SUV with things of value, we could high tail it back up here for a night, and early in the morning light out for Idaho and a life free of Government interference. Live like free Americans and tell all the rest of these crackers to kiss our asses."

The rest of the morning was spent cleaning and loading weapons; packing the Explorer with any type of tool they had to help in their so-called mission.

Sweat dripped off Muscle's brow, more out of nervousness than warmth. As they headed out of the mountains, Sheena and Steele plus the pups stared from a cliff above the campground.

Sheena whispered to Steele, "I have a bad sense about these two. I don't think we're rid of them any time soon."

"Be patient my mate, this pair looks weak and soft, and should offer no problem if we decided to attack."

Without another word or sound of any kind, the wolf pack turned and padded up the worn trail.

Forty

"The dart entered her right hind leg above the knee in the fleshy part of her thigh. Falen jumped when the sting hit but thought something like an insect had bitten her. She turned her head back to bite at the area hoping the pain would go away. It didn't. In fact the area of the first sting on her leg started to grow and become hot. A remarkable thing then happened. The pain started to immediately disappear and her entire leg became numb. The numbness spread up to her back and soon she barely held her head up.

"I'm so helpless. What can this be? Oh, Spirit of the Day and Night, protect me from this terrible hurt."

In a matter of minutes she sank into a dark place not quite sleep but total unconsciousness. She felt no pain, no sense of being alive, just darkness.

The headache was tremendous and woke her from the comatose state. Falen tried to move her legs but they were taped together, front and back. The floor of the car under her was hard with a huge bump pushing up into her ribs. Disoriented, she gulped in air to identify her condition. The smell of tobacco and human body odor alerted her to the danger, but at the moment she couldn't figure out how to escape. The one thing she did know was to lay still and trust in the Spirit of the Day and Night to save her.

"I'm glad we grabbed that soldier's dog. We'll teach her some manners. She'll be a little less eager thinking she can attack people like us."

"What are we going to do with her?" Muscles stared out the front window trying to navigate the tiny road carved through with potholes. The Explorer bounced around like a toy truck.

Weiner held on to the strap above the passenger door and braced himself with his left hand planted on the dashboard. All of the vibration made his voice shaky, "Well, uh, I mean, we might sell her to one of them research hospitals for them to carve her up. Hey, look out! You nearly tumped this thing over, uh, but back to the damned dog. Let's take her to Idaho with us, and let some of our patriot brothers use her for bait in their dog fighting pits."

Muscles grinned through his clenched teeth as he tried to guide the four-wheel drive SUV over and around some fallen trees.

As soon as the road leveled, he said, "Oh man, a fighting pit would serve that she- devil right for attacking a human being. Once one of them Pit dogs got ahold of her, she would rue the day she thought she could bite us."

Falen's mouth wasn't taped, only her legs, so she was able to try to loosen the bindings without making enough noise to attract the attention of the men.

"Do you see the green SUV down there trying to make it over all the crap in the way on the old fire road."

The hiker's companion peered at the vehicle through his binoculars, "Yeah, who- ever is driving must not know these mountains very well. At the end of the road is a cliff dropping nearly straight down. One of the reasons why the Forest Service closed it after the terrible blizzard we had several years back. The snowmelt washed the road away. I hope he's aware of the danger before he gets a rude awaking."

"Remember the crude campsite we passed? Maybe that's theirs and they don't intend to go all the way to the end of the road."

The first hiker passed the binoculars back adding, "Listen with all the weirdo's seeking refuge in these mountains, who can tell what this group is up to." Both continued to watch the green Explorer inch its way through the debris. Finally the man spoke, "I think its best we leave these guys alone."

All of a sudden the SUV stopped about fifty feet down from the rickety campsite.

"Hold on a minute, what are they doing now?"

Weiner and Muscles exited the car and opened the back door.

"Here, give me a hand carrying this damned dog. She sure must eat good. She weighs a ton."

Muscles grabbed Falen's bound back legs and pulled, wrestling Falen out. Weiner waited until the dog's body was over half way out, and latched on to her front legs. Falen stayed quiet. This was no time to try to fight back. She had to trust and hope an escape was possible.

The two men stumbled and fought their way up the side of the incline toward their campsite.

"Hells Bells, Weiner, let's drop this mutt here and let her die. I can't believe how heavy she is."

Weiner answered through clenched teeth. Nope, let's make it up to the site and we'll decide what to do. I would love to give her a swift kick in the ribs for all she put us through."

Forty-One

Sergio was having the time of his life. Many of his fellow ranchers and friends from church stopped by the Gonzales clan's table. He wrapped up a "tall tale", holding everyone at the table spellbound, when his cell phone began ringing and vibrating on the table. While the others laughed at his story, he answered the call with a simple " "Hola".

"Mr. Sergio, this is Hal. I am sorry to bother you all but something has happened on the ranch you need to know about."

Waving for the folks to be quiet, Sergio said, "Go on, Hal," he straightened up in his chair, "What's the matter?"

The concern on the elder Gonzales face spoke volumes to Rick and Isabelle. Susan stiffened. She reached over for Rick's hand.

Hal continued on the phone, "Well sir, I was lying down for a nap when I hear a car running in the drive way in front of your house."

The rancher's squinted up his eyes preparing for the bad news.

"I rounded the back corner of the house and saw two no-good lookin' men carrying Falen to their van." He paused for a moment and continued. "She appeared lifeless with her head hanging. The men threw her in the back seat and drove off in one hell of a hurry."

Sergio met Rick's eyes and nodded. "We'll be right home."

"What is it Dad? What's going on?"

"Come on you guys, something has happened to Falen, and we have to get home quick."

On the way out Rick bumped into Deputy Hampton coming in the front door.

"Tommy, follow us home, there's been a robbery and we think someone kidnapped Falen."

A take-charge guy, Sergio jumped into the driver's seat of Rick's Sequoia as Susan and Isabelle got into the back. Rick rode shotgun with Tommy Hampton's cruiser leading the way. On the way back to the ranch Sergio related all Hal told him to everyone. Isabelle and Susan clinched the back of the seat in front. Each woman's heart raced.

The Sweetgrass Sheriff's Department patrol car skidded to a stop followed closely by Rick's SUV and Park County deputy, Lew Manuel. As soon as Tommy found out the vehicle in question was a Green Explorer an all-points bulletin was issued. Deputy Lew Manuel was near the Gonzales ranch and answered the call. Hal stood on the porch anxious to fill in the details of his encounter with the robbers.

"Nothing else seems to be stolen or disturbed." Deputy Hampton came back out front after a quick inspection of the interior of the house with Isabelle.

Rick squeezed Susan's hand, the veins in his neck almost standing at attention. All of his war training prepared him for moments like this. While calm on the outside he churned inside.

"Where do you think these men took her?" Sergio gazed up into the mountains as if he were trying to spot her.

"I tell you Mr. Gonzales, if it was the two we've been searching for they hide out somewhere in the National Forest."

Rick chimed in, "That's a lot of ground to cover."

"It's not like we've not been searching," Deputy Manuel stated, "We've been on a wild goose chase ever since they started trouble with those campers several months ago."

"They picked up the green Explorer a week back from those tourists at Paradise Gateway."

Lew pulled a picture of the car from his folder, "This is a picture of the car, and of course, this picture shows it loaded down with the Simons' traveling things. I'm pretty sure it's a lot different now.

We should start a search party as soon as we can. I'll inform the other agencies, and Mr. Gonzales, if you would call a lot of your rancher friends who are familiar with the high mountain ranges maybe they could join us as a search party?"

Rick kept clenching and unclenching his hands. Finally he exploded, "You all do what you think is right, but I'm heading out right now. I'm going to take the four-wheeler; I can't stand to think of her alone and scared. I'm taking my pistol as well. I've got a two-way mounted in the dash. Dad, you know the frequency so I'll be listening. But I'm not spending another minute without making a personal effort to find her."

With that he grabbed his heavy coat, turned and headed out to the shed where the ATV was kept.

Forty-Two

"You lazy bastard, stop drinking up all our beer and get your butt over here and help me pile more branches on this damn car."

Muscles did the most work trying to camouflage the vehicle just in case helicopters flew overhead trying to spot them.

"Leave enough room for us to get in if'n we need to leave in a hurry."

Some areas of the mountains get dark a lot quicker when the sun sets over the peaks. Weiner figured they had about an hour of good daylight before the forest around them became dark.

"Let's build a smaller fire tonight in case any of them locals are trying to find us."

"Black as the night gets up here no one will ever find this location. Tomorrow, first thing, we'll be gone and headed for Idaho. If we have to get out of here, I'll just shoot the damned dog. Serves her right, anyway."

Falen could sense from the tone of the conversation her immediate danger. Earlier in the afternoon, Weiner had taken a large limb and beat her with it. She held her voice, and didn't yelp or whine even though the pain was unbearable. Ever since the beating she had an immense pain in her right rear leg and even though she was only bound around the neck she had trouble standing up.

The thin rope Muscles used to tie her was knotted so if she pulled hard trying to get away, the noose tightened, making it hard to get her breath.

She kept an eye on the two men as they piled more and more brush on the car.

"Oh Spirit of the Day and Night, please help me be strong and not afraid. Let me be watchful and vigilant, so I can find a way to escape. Make me mindful of your help as I cry out to you for mercy."

Above the campsite Sheena and Steele stood guard as the humans worked. The frantic nature of the pair aroused the curiosity of both wolves. Sheena especially stared at the dog tied to the tree. Something was familiar about the dog. Then it dawned on the Wolf dog that this was Bandit's littermate. Sheena remembered her from the times she prowled above Javier Coronado's ranch spying on Bandit.

Now she was doubly apprehensive of the outsiders. What were they doing with Bandit's sister? The whole affair smelled of danger. Sheena stood hidden in the trees without making a sound. Her time would come.

With dusk falling over the area, Rick had two extra strong headlamps, plus the saddlebags contained flares if he needed them. He had prowled these mountainsides since childhood, and knew the area better than a lot of the forest rangers. His heart beat faster and faster. He had to find his dog. She wasn't alone. The Marine Corp motto 'never leave a buddy behind' was all too real for the Corporal. Nothing mattered except finding Falen.

"Falen, Falen, where are you girl?" Rick alternated calling her name and whistling. The headlights knifed through the deep forest. He sniffed the air trying to find any trace of smoke from a campfire.

"I know this is a foolish mission out here in the dark, but I can't stand to think of her afraid and abused, and me not being with her to comfort and protect."

Somehow his nerves were soothed voicing the words out loud.

"Hell, if it wasn't for her I wouldn't be here now. She brought me though the dark times, and with the help of Susan led me back among the living. I have to find her, I have to save her, Falen is such an important part of me."

The ATV bounced over a fallen log nearly unseating Rick. He stopped the four-wheeler and listened to the silence of the night, hoping for any sound that could lead him to his dog.

The hours drew on as Rick pushed his vehicle up the mountain side, looking on each and every fire road. All he thought about was Falen, and the more he thought about the situation the more afraid he became.

Forty-Three

The dusk faded into night. Preparations began all over the three-county area, as law enforcement agencies believed the objects of their search were being drawn into their noose.

Sergio and Hal worked the phones at the ranch asking for volunteers to join the rescue attempt for Falen.

Sergio dialed the number for his old friend, Javier Coronado. On the second ring he answered. "Hello."

"Javier, this is Sergio and I have some terrible news."

Javier started to speak but his old friend continued.

"Someone stole Falen. We got back to the ranch and she was gone. Hal said a green SUV pulled out of our drive in one hell of a hurry. We assumed Falen was inside.

The Sheriff's office believes the two culprits are holed up in the mountains somewhere in the National forest. We're going to need as many warm bodies as we can get to comb these mountains. You are as familiar with the high country as anyone." Javier interrupted, "Of course. What I will do is get up about 3am and get my feeding done, then take Bayo and Bandit and we'll search the area away from the main roads. On Bayo I can move quickly and with Bandit Boy's great nose, we will be doubly affective."

"Thank you, mi amigo. I can always count on you."

Bandit sensed something wrong, and stood at Javier's feet, ears up and alert, awaiting orders."

Javier rubbed the Aussie's dark head and peered into the depths of his eyes, murmuring, "I can always depend on you old Friend. We've been through a lot, and now our Falen girl needs our help."

"Whoa, Bandit", as the big black dog scooted for the front door. "We must rest now, and get an early start, but remember, we must put out hay for the cows and feed our other dogs."

Bandit's eyes focused on the face of his master taking in every word.

"Once we leave, we won't be back until we find our Falen girl. A lump arose in Javier's throat when he thought he might never see the little red dog again.

"Your father, Warner, will help guide us on our way."

"And the Spirit of the Day and Night will protect us, and Falen until she can safely return," Bandit said in a series of chirps and mini barks.

Deputy Manuel stopped at a gas station to fill up before the long night of searching. A Volkswagen van plastered with travel stickers pulled up alongside and two weathered, but attractive people got out and approached the patrol car.

"Excuse me, Officer, but we're in the need of some good direction," The man grinned, "Are you the travel direction deputy here in Park County?"

Lew chuckled, "They've called me a lot of things, but travel direction deputy is a new one." He topped off the tank and replaced the hose, "Now what kind of help or direction do you need."

"We've been hiking around these mountains for about seven days or so. The area is probably one of the most beautiful we've been in."

Lew Manuel pointed out all of the travel stickers and said, "All of those stickers say you've been in a lot of areas."

"Oh yes, we've spent the better part of three summers touring, loving every minute. But we want to cross over the mountains and we noticed when you get off of the main path on some of these older roads you can run into a lot of trouble."

The young woman chimed in, "We were up on the mountain this afternoon and a fire road someone was using had been damaged by, I guess flooding waters, and was completely washed out.

We were far enough away the folks in the car wouldn't have heard our shouts if we tried, but fortunately for them they stopped before the road ran out. They turned off the road and drove into the trees."

Her companion picked up the story, "That green Explorer was bounding around like crazy over rocks and logs in the road. I thought if they got too close to the end of the road, and weren't careful they might have slipped right over the edge."

Deputy Manuel's eyes squinted at the mention of the Green SUV. His attention sharpened.

"Can you point out on a map the area you were in?"

Both young people caught the Deputy's change in tone.

"Why? Do you know those two?"

"Let's put it this way, I want to know them a lot better, if they are the two we've been searching for in a stolen Green Ford Explorer. I need to meet them real soon, the sooner the better?"

Lew grabbed a pad from his cruiser and took copious notes as the young hikers drew a picture of where they had seen the car last.

They added, "Something else funny, they dragged what looked like a dead dog out of the car and up an embankment." He paused, "I thought it was strange." The girl spoke up, "Me too. Why would someone carry a dead dog along with them."

Forty-Four

Falen wasn't dead, but close to it. Her heart missed beats as she gasp for air. The noose around her neck tightened with the slightest movement.

The slimmest of moonlight filtered through the branches of the tall trees creating dances of light adding to the mystery of the night. The fire pit burned down to an ember. Muscles and Weiner had passed out on the ground failing to cover up with their sleeping bags. Fully dressed they had packed the SUV with the loot they had stolen during the day, and were ready for an early getaway as soon as morning broke.

It didn't dawn on them that the cover of night would have been perfect for an elusive retreat. They had operated openly in the day as if they were invisible.

Nothing moved and no sound cut the darkness except for the muted murmurings of pain from Falen.

She prayed, *"Oh Spirit of the Day and Night, if I must die here, please let me die without pain. I know I will join my mother and our friends over the rainbow bridge. I am not afraid of dying, but I dread the pain."*

As the words slipped from her mind she heard a voice.

"Don't be afraid little one, I am here to protect you and give you freedom."

Falen's eyes snapped open. Was she dreaming? Did the Spirit of the Day and Night answer her? Her nose filled with the warm scent of musk and life. Opposite from the stench of the men who held her captive This was the odor of mother's milk and security. The first thing she saw were golden eyes peering out of the darkness, illuminated by the last embers of the fire just above her and near enough for the creature's scent to cascade down over her snout. The breath of life was filling her nose. It boosted her hope and drove out despair.

"Little Falen girl, I am Sheena, Bandit's other mother. I watched the men who put you in this distress, and waited until I might save you and help you home."

The red head moved against the binding rope to search for the mighty wolf she had learned so much about from her mother and Bandit.

"Lay still, my baby. Don't move and let me try to chew this twine in two."

Sheena had crawled from her hiding place on her stomach so that her head rested near the stricken dog. With her mighty wolf teeth she sawed and severed the rope freeing Falen's neck.

"Stand up my child, let us be ever so quiet, and slip away from these men."

Falen rose up on her front legs, but couldn't put any weight on her right rear. The simple task of standing up, that had always come so natural to her, now became an unbearable task. She realized her right side didn't work properly. When she rolled over to let the left hind leg take the brunt of the pressure she could stand, but was still in excruciating pain. She bit down so hard she nearly punctured her tongue, but it helped keep her from yelping out and awaking the sleeping men.

Sheena used her body to help prop up Falen and ease some of the pressure on the broken leg. The beating she had taken fractured her rear leg. It hadn't broken in two but pain cascaded up and down her limb with the slightest movement. Leaning on Sheena's strong body, Falen hobbled her way into the depths of the woods, where she would be hidden from the humans. A slight crunching of the leaves on the floor of the forest caused Muscles to roll over, but the effects of his drunken state let him dissolve back into deep sleep. Weiner never moved.

Sheena's eyes, used to the deep darkness, enabled Falen to let her lead the way, all the while leaning closer and closer to the great wolf's side. Falen kept up with Sheena and moved step by step, ever mindful of the danger if the human's awoke.

Brushes hit Falen's face, causing her to depend more and more on Sheena. Once her front paw slipped on a fallen log, causing her to lose her balance. She fought to keep the cries of pain in her mind, and not let them out. One outburst and the trouble would start again.

Forty-Five

"Lew, we've passed out the walkie-talkies to all of the volunteers and instructed them how to dial in the frequency so we all can be on the same channel."

Tommy Hampton stepped out from his patrol car to give his legs a stretch by standing up for a moment.

"The only person we missed was Javier Coronado who, according to Sergio left about 3:00a.m. on his gelding. Sergio has Javier's radio contact and will pass along the coordinates."

"Tommy, you got the scoop on our perps I passed along from those hikers?"

"Roger. I also passed the info on to all of the volunteers warning them the suspects are armed and considered extremely dangerous."

"I am heading out in one of the Department's four-wheelers. I'll stay on the radio. You be safe out there. Call if you need backup."

"Roger, Lew. Stay safe."

"Easy old man, you're getting a little wobbly. Bandit can jump over these logs but that doesn't mean you and I have to. We can step lightly. Bandit's not going to leave us."

Bandit had 'radared' in on the mission. His heart remained in communion with the Spirit of the Day and Night, so Bandit needed no urging to place saving Falen first over everything else.

Bandit's black head swung right and left, sampling the air for any familiar scent or sign of danger. The Morgan Gelding placed each hoof in a secure spot, careful not to unseat his master. Bandit made sure he never got too far out of sight.

The radio on Javier's belt crackled. "Javier, this is Deputy Hampton, come in, over."

The rancher pushed the talk button. "Coronado here, come back."

Bayo paused and listened for the tone of his master's voice.

Bandit stopped up ahead at the crackle of the radio and returned to stand by the side of the horse.

"Sir, we've narrowed the search for the two wanted men down to an area off the main forest road into some very heavy woods. I am advising the entire search team to be extra careful. These men are armed and exceedingly dangerous. If you spot the camp, do not, I repeat, do not go in alone."

"I got it, Deputy. When I see them I will radio you."

"Thanks, over and out."

The old Basque herdsman sat still while the message he just heard played through his thoughts. He patted the horse's neck to soothe his restlessness. Both horse and dog were attuned to the danger of this search. They must perform at an intense level of awareness, keeping the safety of the old rancher foremost on their minds.

The first pink line of light appeared in the east and the wind picked up over the mountains and slashed through the trees causing a whistling sound. Muscles was the first to be awakened by the sound. He sat straight up rubbing his eyes trying to focus on the surroundings.

"Weiner, get up, man. We've got to get goin'. It'll be full daylight in an hour or so, and I'm sure half the county is out looking for us. If'n we don't leave pretty soon, we may start camping out in the local hoosegow."

"Gimme a minute here, would'ya. My head hurts so bad I think I'll go blind."

"Get downwind from me, boy, your breath would melt iron."

Muscles turned around and exclaimed, "Holy Shit! Look at this. The damned dog chewed through the rope and is gone. I bet she couldn't go far with her gimpy leg you gave her with the stick you hit her with. Let's try and catch her."

"Why don't we just leave her be, get our stuff, and get our asses out of here? She is trouble! I guarantee it."

Weiner stood up and followed his partner a little way into the woods. "Like I said man, let's get on gone, leave all this trouble behind us and head for our Patriot town in Idaho."

Stopping and turning around to stare at the disheveled Weiner, Muscles chided, "And leave money just running through the woods. If I told you once I told you a hundred times, those boys of ours pay a good amount for the bait dogs. Shit, we can make plenty off a selling the bitch, plus we can gamble on how long she's going to last. Let's get going. She ain't gonna be hard to find."

Forty-Six

The Timber Wolf stuck his snout up in the air to determine the direction of the nauseating scents filling his nose.

Remaining hidden behind a giant boulder and thick underbrush he kept alert to the movement of the humans since Sheena had left on her mission of mercy with Bandit Dog's sister. Steele didn't worry about his pups. They wouldn't leave the den without permission. Of that he was sure. Yet, he remained wary as the putrid odor of these men engulfed him from the prevailing wind.

Steele had never attacked a human. Sheena shared the story of her encounter with the man who brutalized her so, but Steele avoided contact with men at all costs.

The sounds of the humans thrashing about between the trees and shouting when their legs tangled in the underbrush grew closer. Steele was determined not to give an inch and to charge if necessary.

The stench got stronger. A loud clap of thunder reverberated throughout the forest. A single drop of rain splashed on the Timber Wolf's muzzle. It was soon followed by a drenching outburst of rain. The two outlaws cursed and ran back to the campsite for cover.

"Damn, Muscles, we're going to get drenched. The damned bitch will have to stay lost. If'n we don't get out of here soon we won't be able to make it down these mountain roads."

The clouds appeared to open right over the campsite. The rain came down in sheets, swirling because of the down draft of the winds over the higher mountain peaks.

Visibility was hampered not only because of the stinging rain, but also because of the strength of the wind blowing the rain even harder into their faces.

Muscles was drenched. His wet hair was plastered to his forehead, his jaws clenching and unclenching as he spoke, "I am going to give one more look at the trail. That red bitch of a dog might come back with all of this rain."

He didn't wait for Weiner to say yea or nay, he turned and hurried up the trail. He rounded the first upward turn of the path and stepped into some heavy brush and brambles.

"Come here you red devil of a dog, come here, so we can go. I'm not going to hurt you. It was damned ole Weiner who gave you a beatin'. Come on now, here, pooch, here pooch."

Muscles sensed something move in the underbrush just ahead. He realized he had no weapon with him so he stooped over and picked up a good size limb.

"I don't care who are what you are, come at me, and I will beat the snot out of you."

The rain caused a dense curtain, obstructing his view to only a couple of yards. With the heavy stick held high over his head, he walked a few steps into the brush.

Steele took his advance as a threat and lunged all of his 140 pounds directly at the human's chest. The blow knocked Muscles down but not before he swung the heavy wood toward the attacker's head. He missed. Steele bounced back snarling. His teeth bared in a furious guttural cry. Muscles managed to get back up and swing with all of his might at the wolf. No blows landed as Steel twisted out of the way, bounced on his four feet and grabbed for the man's leg.

Wolves can bite down at 1500 pounds per inch, much greater than the strongest dog's bite. Muscles leg, gripped in the strong jaws of the Timber Wolf, was torn so quickly he didn't notice the pain, at first. His blood mingled with the soaking rain and ran down into his shoe. Steele loosened his grip, freeing the mangled limb and backed up to charge again if he had to.

Weiner heard the screams of his partner and rushed to help. Muscles was standing now, his pant leg severed, and a gaping wound in his thigh.

He kept screaming. Wiener spied the giant wolf and screeched to a halt. Torn between running to save himself, and rescuing his friend. Weiner stared at the wolf in horror. Speechless, he remained rooted to the spot, not moving and not being able to run away.

Muscles, torn leg and all, ran on sheer adrenaline, nearly knocking Wiener down as he passed. Weiner couldn't take his eyes off of the deadly wolf. He backed up about six or seven steps. The Wolf didn't advance. With an exhale of air, the frightened man turned his back to the dangerous animal and ran as fast as he could back to the campsite.

"Help me man, I can't stop this bleeding." Muscles grasped at the torn rope used to tie up Falen, and tried to make a tourniquet above the gash in his right leg. Weiner stood over him frozen. Mounting his courage, he glanced back up the path to see if the wolf had come closer. When nothing moved in the distance, he came to his senses and bent down to help his fallen Militiaman.

"Let's get the hell out of here, man. We need to get out of this forest and get on our way to Idaho."

Screw all of this shit we haven't loaded. Let's get in the car and head out of this God-forsaken place."

"Help me. I don't think I can walk."

Wiener eased an arm around the wounded man, letting Muscles rest his right side on him as they hobbled toward the car and safety.

Forty-Seven

The deluge created hazardous conditions for anybody moving through the high forest, whether on horseback or ATV.

Rick tried to balance himself as the front tires of the ATV slid off a huge rock in the middle of the path. The four-wheeler grasped the slippery surface, but the front right tire lost its traction throwing the vehicle off balance and nearly over the edge of a gully.

"Hold on, damn you" Rick shouted, "Let's not turn over here."

The marine's hands held onto the steering wheel in a death grip, and because of his artificial leg, he wasn't able to push himself enough to try to balance the weight. His foot on the prosthetic didn't feel the floor, just the pressure he was exerting trying to stay upright.

"Rick, this is Javier do you read me?" The front right tire grabbed the surface of the boulder in time for the ATV to stabilize. Rick stopped and grabbed for his radio attached to his belt.

"Yes, Javier, I read you. What's going on?

"What is your location?"

Rick glanced around the area to get his bearings. The light of dawn was faint due to the amount of rain falling from the heavy clouds overhead.

"I seem to be about 20 miles northwest of your ranch. The twin peaks are off in the distance, which if I calculate correctly, would put me near the high meadow, but still in the woods downhill."

"I must be about 30 minutes ahead of you. I can hear a truck starting and I don't believe it's from any of our volunteers."

"Be careful, Javier. You remember what Tommy radioed about these guys being armed and dangerous."

"I am moving very slowly now due to the wet conditions." He chuckled, "Even Bandit doesn't seem to like these conditions. But if the rain would slow down the wet air improves his scenting."

"Whoa, Bayo, settle down." Javier stopped. He pushed the talk button again, "I am going to slow down and let you catch up. If you are south of the pasture, loop down about 500 feet and you will hit the new fire road. Follow it and you will find me pretty soon."

Park County Deputy Lew Manuel rounded a bend in the road when the ignition of a car grabbed his attention. On alert Manuel tried to position the sound in relation to his location.

The noise of the car grew louder, but the sound indicated the vehicle was still quite far away. Sounds travel faster in the mountains, especially with a low ceiling of clouds. Manuel lowered the volume on his radio. A blast from a car horn sounded. He looked in the direction and decided he was up about a thousand feet from the noise appearing to be just to his left. He moved to the edge of a cliff for a better view. Down about 400 hundred yards below a Green Explorer was slipping and sliding along the old fire road the hikers had indicated that they had seen the suspects. The spinning wheels caused a high whine with the car bouncing off of logs and rocks, but the Deputy couldn't locate them.

"Goddamn it, Weiner, you are going to get us kilt. Watch out for that log. Oh, Hell's Bells, man, we're going to fall right off the side of this shitty road."

Weiner stayed silent. The accidental blast from the horn unnerved him. Focusing all of his attention and strength on keeping the SUV in the middle of the road, he knew he was driving too fast, but the danger of being caught drove him on at reckless speeds.

The steering wheel slipped in his muddy hands causing the front tires to veer to the right. He whipped his hands to the left trying to straighten up the motion. Instead, he caused the rear tires to spin dangerously close to the right side of the road. The car straightened for a moment when the treads seized a rocky part of the dirt road. Steering away from the right, he caused the nose of the car to slam in the opposite direction, dangerously close to spinning out of control. A gust of wind slammed the windshield with excess water.

He reached for the cloth to wipe the glass, letting go with one hand. The car accelerated, yanking the steering wheel out of his hands. He had little time to try to apply the brakes, when he saw the washed out road ahead. The brakes only served to cause the car to lock its wheels, causing the car to spin out of control. Weiner screamed. He gripped the steering wheel with one hand, and reached for the roof with the other. Both men's mouths gaped open with silent screams as the Explorer flipped over and over falling and bouncing off the rocks and sides of the steep incline. As the van settled in the rocks upside down, the force of the impact rendered them unconscious. The rear jammed into a crevice in the rocks with the nose pointing back up toward the road. All noise stopped. It became deadly quiet with only the sound of the decreasing rain bouncing off the frame of the Green Explorer.

Forty-Eight

The throbbing pain radiated from her broken leg up into her spine and made the use of her good left leg almost impossible. Falen let out a small whine. Sheena leaned closer to her adopted daughter to stabilize her and help with movement. Sheena's heart broke as she experienced little Falen's anguish. The slippery ground made walking even difficult for the Wolf Dog.

A groan from deep in the Aussies bowels escaped from her clenched teeth.

"Easy my baby, it won't be long and we will be back to your home."

Words of comfort spoken softly, almost in a whisper, eased Falen's trouble mind. Sheena feared the humans who caused all of this pain were following. Yet she feared if they picked up the pace, considerable damage might occur to the red Aussie's leg, possibly leaving her crippled for life.

Each step caused excruciating pain. Canines don't cry like people, but the stress made Falen's eyes water, and the ache caused her to squint, making her vision all the more impaired. The rain slowed, allowing Sheena to quicken her step trying to balance the injured dog on her side.

"Dear Spirit of the Day and Night, allow my strength to be sufficient, not only for me, but also for my adopted daughter, who is in such agony. Protect us and give us succor during this trying time."

Falen's heart filled with the prayers of the mighty Timber wolf. She had learned of Sheena's great love for her brother, Bandit, and now was assured of the wolf dog's love for her. Falen murmured over and over, *"Thank you."*

Rick pulled his field glasses from the fanny pack and focused on the wilderness ahead. His ears attuned for any sound, he searched the landscape looking for Javier and hoping to find Falen. Off in the distance as the sun finally broke through the clouds, he thought he made out a man on horseback. Focusing and re-focusing the binoculars, his heart sank. It was just a bull moose ambling through the woods. Cold and wet, he wiped the lens, and swung his surveillance more to the left. An opening appeared in the wall of trees. Something was moving up ahead, and Rick was sure this time it wasn't a moose. A dark speck ran in front followed by the familiar form of Javier Coronado and his gelding Bayo. Rick stifled a shout knowing the distance was too much for sound to carry, and not wanting to alarm the outlaws of their presence. A Medevac helicopter hovered over the deeper part of the mountain's side about two miles to the right. Rick took a chance and gunned the motor, propelling the ATV over the rocky terrain.

"I've got you. Can you make out what's down there?"

"Roger, Deputy. It's a green SUV at the bottom, just over the cliff. It's pretty torn up. Nothing is moving and it seems a long way down. I have a hoist on board and my co-pilot can be lowered down to the scene for a look-around. Over."

Lew Manuel leaned up on the front of the Park County's ATV peering down the deadly drop off. "If you can do it, safely. Remember, they are considered armed and dangerous, so please don't take any chances. From where I am now, it seems awfully quiet."

"Deputy Hampton, can you copy?"

"Got you Lew, what' up?"

"I think our bad guys went off the deep end, literally. I think they're trapped in the wreckage. A Montana State rescue copter currently circling the scene advised his co- pilot could ferry down a hoist. What are your thoughts?"

"Before those medics attempt a rescue, let me check with the Sheriff and find out how they want this thing handled. The last thing we need is some shot up Medics, who are just trying to help." "I'll let them circle around while we decide. If anything comes up, I'll give a holler. Let's get some backup headed in this general direction. Any word on Rick's lost dog?"

"Nothing to speak of. Listen for Rick on his two way."

Forty-Nine

Javier was transfixed staring at the strange site up about 300 yards on the break of the mountains. He wiped his eyes with his bandana, and strained for a clearer view. The old rancher believed he was staring at least two animals, but the way they seemed to be moving made it appear to be one. He stood up in the stirrups to get a better view. Bandit swung his head around trying to catch a faint familiar scent on the wind flowing down from the higher elevation.

"What ya looking at, Mister Coronado?" Javier turned in the saddle as Rick's ATV pulled up to a stop.

"Look over here, Rick. Doesn't it appear like two animals, possible dogs or wolves, walking slowly down the side of the hill?"

"Let me put my binoculars on them". Rick rummaged in his fanny back for the glasses. Bandit changed his position. The big dog's ears snapped to attention and he let out a series of barks, loud enough to reach the moon.

The pair on the hill stopped in their tracks. Bandit proceeded to bark even louder followed by a period of quiet. He held his head steady straining for an answer of any kind.

"I think it's either two wolves, one large one and another smaller, or it might be dogs. I can't tell. They remain so close together."

Neither man spoke allowing only Bandit's barking to fill the void.

Then it came, a lonely howl only a wolf in distress can make. The wail filled the air with such a mournful plea all the other animals in the forest seemed to stop and listen.

Deep within his being Bandit shivered. He recognized the howl; a cry of help sent to the rest of the pack when a lone wolf is in danger. Rick and Javier didn't believe their ears. The black Aussie threw back his head, and produced a howl only a wolf could make.

"Mother, I am here, your Bandit. I will come as quickly as possible to your side. Fear not, your son is coming. I will save you from all danger."

Bandit leaped forward and ran as quickly as his legs would take him toward the high part of the hill where the stranded wolf stood.

Javier and Rick remained motionless.

"I don't think we should follow him too closely."

"Me neither, Javier. Let's not approach the animals. We'll know soon enough whether or not he's in danger."

The Basque herdsman patted the 30-06 he kept in a saddle scabbard assuring himself of its reach.

"You go on up on horseback. I will stay close enough that I can speed up if necessary." With that Rick powered down the ATV and Javier headed out.

"Oh, Sheena, that's Bandit's bark. He's come to help us. O Spirit of the Day and Night you've sent our salvation. And it's my brother, Bandit."

Sheena didn't answer. As was her nature she remained cautious; ever alert in case this wasn't what she thought. Her attention remained fixated on the black dog bounding over the terrain, leaping logs, bouncing off boulders, racing toward them. She raised her voice again and called a greeting. Bandit answered, still running at full speed. Two high-pitched yelps were music to the wolf dog's ears. She allowed herself a moment of explosive joy. The closer Bandit drew to the stranded pair the more she shook with delight. Falen was too weak to join in the chorus of gleeful yelps and chirps. She was nearly pushed over by the exuberance of the Wolf's welcome for her adopted son. As he drew closer, the quieter the yelps became until when Bandit was about 20 yards away. Sheena was whining cries of joy. Sheena couldn't move to greet him afraid she would unbalance Falen, and cause her even more pain.

Then it came, nose-to-nose. Bandit and Sheena reunited. She covered his face with licks of adoration. He caressed her neck and shoulder as a puppy would a returning mother. He moaned and groaned with love for this great wolf. The Mother who saved him in the storm, and raised him with all the wiles of animals born to a life in the wilderness.

Sheena enjoyed the Aussie's tenderness and devotion.

"My mother, my Sheena, it is I, Bandit, whose heart is always entwined with yours." He paused and turned his attention on his sister. Weak, she nearly fell over trying to stretch her neck toward her beloved brother.

"Bandit, oh my Bandit, I knew you would come. In my prayers to the Spirit of the Day and Night, I had the assurance of your protection. Now you are here. I love you so, and I am so thankful the Spirit of the Day and Night answered my pleas."

Bandit stood next to the wolf and his sibling. No one spoke, nothing moved. A voice broke the silence, "Bandit my dog, all is safe. I am coming to your side."

The human voice startled Sheena; she hadn't heard a person speak in love in a long time. She recognized the old Shepherd, and now that Bandit was here, she removed herself from the immediate area, backing out about fifteen paces.

This allowed the other human, Rick, to advance to the scene. He moved in step by step, not wanting to cause any sudden excuse for the beautiful Timber Wolf to flee.

As he reached Falen tears streamed down his face. The Marine's arms encircled the red head of his dog and he nuzzled his face into her fur. Falen collapsed in his arms. His words broke with emotion as he stroked the Red Tri's body again and again.

"Semper Fi my little one, always faithful. You were there for me in my hours of despair, and now I am here for you. Semper Fi describes our love, one for the other. We never leave a comrade behind."

Javier dismounted and stood by his dog, Bandit. His hand ruffled the black fur and his fingers caressed the Aussie's ears.

"Semper Fi. Those are good words to describe the heart of man and dog. Semper Fi, my Bandit.

Falen's final tale.

It's been nearly a year since I began this conversation. I still love to lounge on the front porch in the warm Montana sunshine, but I've grown a lot in the past 12 months. Learning about myself, my family, and what is important in this life and what isn't.

People say how important dogs are to the healing process of not only wounded warriors, but to all who suffer from extreme stress or pain. I've experienced pain and lived through it, which makes me understand the early days when Rick first came home, how his suffering overwhelmed him.

As you can tell, I am laying on the front porch of an entirely different house from Sergio's ranch house. I can see the house from my perch, but proudly, this is Rick and Susan's new house. Well, mine too, to be exact.

I got to be the ring bearer when those two got married. I tried to carry the ring box in my mouth, but kept dropping the box whenever I barked with joy. Finally, Sergio tied it around my neck and I was able to chirp and murf all the way down the aisle.

The two outlaws were captured, and by now they are secure in Montana's State Prison system, never to bother us again.

I get to spend time with Bandit, and our Mother, Jenny, now as Rick leaves me with Javier when he and Susan are going to be gone for a while. Why don't Rick's parents take care of me? It's because they bought this huge RV, and spend most of their time traveling, while the new boss of the ranch, Rick, tends to the family business. Susan still works with her father in the insurance agency, but comes home early every day to play with me. She's gotten really good at Frisbee.

Today will start another adventure for me. Rick and Susan promised they are going to take me with them into Livingston for the 4th of July celebration. I am hoping they will bring me a Doggy bag from the Sport restaurant. I like good food, too.

Believe me, I've learned to trust the Spirit of the Day and Night more after my ordeal. Sometimes late in the afternoon, I lope to the edge of the ranch property and wait until I identify my favorite sound. From the edge of the forest, I hear the family howl of a Timber Wolf. Not just any wolf but the reassuring howls of the Mighty Sheena. She is our protector and for this I give all Praise and Glory to the Spirit of the Day and Night.

The End.

The Intrepid Fallen Heroes Fund is a leader in supporting the men and women of the armed forces and their families. Established in 2000, the Fund has provided over $150 million in support for the families of military personnel lost in service to our nation, and for severely wounded service members and veterans. The Fund's most recent effort was construction of the National Intrepid Center of Excellence (NICoE), a $60 million, 72,000 square foot facility dedicated to research, diagnosis and treatment of traumatic brain injury, which afflicts many thousands of veterans of the Iraq and Afghanistan conflicts. In 2013 the Fund launched a new $100 million campaign to build nine NICoE satellite centers at major military bases around the country. Each called "Intrepid Spirit," these satellite centers will extend the care provided at NICoE to more service members and veterans suffering from TBI, PTS and related afflictions. Over $40 million has been raised to date and the first two centers at Fort Belvoir, VA and Camp Lejeune, NC, began operations in July 2013. Two more centers are under construction, at Fort Campbell, KY and Fort Bragg, NC, and raising the remaining $60 million will guarantee that the remaining five centers can be built and put into operation to support our wounded heroes in uniform.

To help this effort please make checks payable to:

INTREPID FALLEN HEROES FUND

One Intrepid Square

West 46th Street & 12th Avenue

New York, NY 10036

Or donate online at:

www.fallenheroesfund.org

For information:

(800) 340-HERO

info@fallenheroesfund.org

Learn more about the Australian Shepherd Dog from the preeminent resource, Jeanne Joy Hartnagle-Taylor.

Jeanne Joy Hartnagle-Taylor was born and raised in in the West. She is from an old pioneer family that traveled to Colorado in covered wagons when it was still a territory. Jeanne Joy is the third of four generations to enjoy a lifetime association with stockdogs. Hartnagle did contract herding work for a number of years. Her experience has taken her on assignment with the Department of Interior to work wild bison bulls with her Australian Shepherds as well as with the United States Department of Agriculture to gather livestock for various inspections. Jeanne trains dogs for practical work and has titled her Aussies in all areas of competition. She has also been in the top ten at the ASCA National Stockdog Finals. Success in training and competitions eventually led to invitations to exhibit her stock-savvy dogs at various livestock events, fairs, and rodeos including the National Western Stock Show and Rodeo in Denver, Colorado and the Amazing World of Dogs at the Meeker Classic Sheepdog Championship Trials. Jeanne Joy also performed at the Livestock Expo in Tepatitlan, Guadalajara, by invitation from the Governor of Jalisco, Mexico. She has judged the European Championships at the Continental Sheepdog Trials in Germany as well as presented training seminars all across North America and Europe.

Jeanne is uniquely qualified to talk about stockdogs and has written for numerous publications such as the Western Horseman Magazine, American Cowboy Magazine and The Cattleman, she has authored several books, including *All About Aussies: The Australian Shepherd from A to Z, Stockdog Savvy, and Greasepaint Matadors: The Unsung Heroes of Rodeo.*

All About Aussies, now in its Fourth Edition was nominated for a Dog Writer's Award, and now we have *Stockdog Savvy*. Additionally, Jeanne is featured in the stockdog training series, Herding I, II, III by Canine Training Systems.

Hartnagle's Las Rocosa Australian Shepherds

Australian Shepherd Club of America's

#1 Hall of Fame Excellent Kennel

www.lasrocosa.com

Tel.: 303-659-6597

49781876R00128

Made in the USA
Charleston, SC
04 December 2015